## Donald MacKenzie and The Murder Room

》》 This title is part of The Murder Room, our series dedicated to making available out-of-print or hard-to-find titles by classic crime writers.

Crime fiction has always held up a mirror to society. The Victorians were fascinated by sensational murder and the emerging science of detection; now we are obsessed with the forensic detail of violent death. And no other genre has so captivated and enthralled readers.

Vast troves of classic crime writing have for a long time been unavailable to all but the most dedicated frequenters of second-hand bookshops. The advent of digital publishing means that we are now able to bring you the backlists of a huge range of titles by classic and contemporary crime writers, some of which have been out of print for decades.

From the genteel amateur private eyes of the Golden Age and the femmes fatales of pulp fiction, to the morally ambiguous hard-boiled detectives of mid twentieth-century America and their descendants who walk our twenty-first century streets, The Murder Room has it all. 》》

## The Murder Room
### Where Criminal Minds Meet

**themurderroom.com**

**Donald MacKenzie 1908–1994**

Donald MacKenzie was born in Ontario, Canada, and educated in England, Canada and Switzerland. For twenty-five years MacKenzie lived by crime in many countries. 'I went to jail,' he wrote, 'if not with depressing regularity, too often for my liking.' His last sentences were five years in the United States and three years in England, running consecutively. He began writing and selling stories when in American jail. 'I try to do exactly as I like as often as possible and I don't think I'm either psychopathic, a wayward boy, a problem of our time, a charming rogue. Or ever was.'

He had a wife, Estrela, and a daughter, and they divided their time between England, Portugal, Spain and Austria.

**Henry Chalice**

Salute from a Dead Man
Death Is a Friend
Sleep Is for the Rich

**John Raven**

Zalenski's Percentage
Raven in Flight
Raven and the Kamikaze
Raven and the Ratcatcher
Raven After Dark
Raven Settles a Score
Raven and the Paperhangers
Raven's Revenge

Raven's Longest Night
Raven's Shadow
Nobody Here By That Name
A Savage State of Grace
By Any Illegal Means
The Eyes of the Goat
The Sixth Deadly Sin
Loose Cannon

**Standalone novels**

Nowhere to Go
The Juryman
The Scent of Danger
Dangerous Silence
Knife Edge
The Genial Stranger
Double Exposure
The Lonely Side of the River
Cool Sleeps Balaban
Dead Straight
Three Minus Two
Night Boat from Puerto Vedra
The Kyle Contract
Postscript to a Dead Letter
The Spreewald Collection
Deep, Dark and Dead
Last of the Boatriders

# Cool Sleeps Balaban

Donald MacKenzie

An Orion book

Copyright © The Estate of Donald MacKenzie 1964

The right of Donald MacKenzie to be identified as the author of this
work has been asserted in accordance with the Copyright, Designs and
Patents Act 1988.

This edition published by
The Orion Publishing Group Ltd
Orion House
5 Upper St Martin's Lane
London WC2H 9EA

An Hachette UK company
A CIP catalogue record for this book is available from the British Library

ISBN 978 1 4719 0575 9

www.orionbooks.co.uk

For Henry and Cyrus – agents, mentors and all too infrequently bankers. With great affection.

# JAMES SCOTT

The first soft flutter of snow drifted across the slapping river. It settled briefly on the headstones, invaded the stunted laurel and iron railings that enclosed the churchyard. Two men stood in the lee of the porch. The darkness of their clothing, the immobility of their pose, robbed them of substance. They were watching the short length of street on the other side of the bushes. It cut south, from the swinging sign outside the corner pub to the narrow apartment building facing the Thames. Midway between these two points, a solitary lamp illuminated the deserted sidewalk and the rear entrance to the apartment building.

The shorter man turned his wrist, checking his watch. He stepped quickly from the shelter of the porch, his voice a cautious whisper.

" Keep your eyes on the back door. He'll be out any moment."

Scott crept forward as far as his cousin's outstretched arm allowed. His hands encased in unfamiliar gloves were sticky. He lifted his head, ignoring the rear entrance, caught by the blazing windows in the penthouse. This crawling, sweating itch to run had been with him ever since they had backed the stolen delivery wagon out of its garage. He'd sat tense beside Craig Usher, his mind creating a roadblock in every quiet Chelsea square. It peopled each passing car with hard-eyed men in trench-coats and black Homburg hats. But the cops sheltering in doorways were real—plainly visible in the flaring traffic signals.

The shadow darkened as Usher became part of it. If he sensed the other's concern, he showed no sign of it. Scott's voice cracked with resentment.

1

"Are you telling me that apartment's empty? Every light in the place is on."

Usher wheeled. He pushed Scott back under the porch. The air there was a compound of stale incense and dank stone.

"That's right," he said evenly. "It's empty."

His own fear needled Scott as much as his cousin's indifference to it.

"You're out of your mind," he said angrily.

Usher let Scott's arm go. "You saw them both get in the cab. I've told you where they've gone for dinner. What do you want to know—the menu?" He blunted the edge of his sarcasm. "Relax, Jamie. Those lights are on because that's the way they like it. And there's no one left up there to turn them off."

It was true enough. They had crouched in the shrubbery, only a few yards from the couple climbing into the cab. Near enough to see the woman's bored mouth and eyes. Maybe Craig was right—maybe these were the sort of people who were not burglar-conscious. Yet Scott's instinct rejected the premise.

A gleam of teeth slashed the outline of Usher's face.

"Nobody's twisting your arm, Jamie, if you want to call it off."

At the end of the concrete path, an unlatched gate gave on the street. All it took was one word. He could walk away from Craig—the stolen wagon and the building in front of them. In a couple of hours he could be home. And then what?

Usher's head was silhouetted against the reflection from the street lamp.

"I mean it, Jamie. I'd be better off alone if you're going to hang crêpe on the deal. What happened to you in two days? You've still got a mortgage—half a dozen horses that can't get out of their own light. You said it, not me— anything that would bail you out of trouble was a proposition."

Scott's stance shifted fractionally. The years had changed neither of them. There was the same spirit of rivalry that went as deep as the bond of affection. He set himself for the blow that could never be struck. He had less control over his tongue.

"It's still a proposition. Don't you remember the first time you ever pulled a stunt like this—or does jail knock it out of your head?"

Usher's answer was quiet. "I remember. You don't know when you're well off, Jamie. Your first and last job's being pulled with a pro. You hit lucky."

The reminder brought small relief. "Luck I don't need," said Scott. "I want a certainty."

Usher was not done. "That's what you're going to get. Do you think I've left anything to chance? While you've been fooling around with horses, I've been in and out of this block half a dozen times. Fitting that apartment with keys —lying in these goddamned bushes till I know every wart on the caretaker's nose."

Scott rebuttoned his overcoat. Words were useless. He pushed by to be first out in the churchyard. They took up position under the stained-glass windows. Snow clung briefly to the boughs of the yew tree on their left, melted on the concrete pathway. Somewhere upstream a tug hooted sadly. Usher grunted as a door slammed beyond the bushes. The watchers bent their heads, peering through the tangle of laurel.

A tall man in raincoat and cloth cap stepped into the lamplight. He managed an over-weight bull terrier on a leash and a pipe with difficulty. The dog snuffled towards the iron stanchion, its claws scrabbling the sidewalk. The man stared hard at the lowering sky, took a swift look up the street and booted the dog squarely in the backside. He was whistling as it scurried after him on his way to the pub.

Usher's hand flashed the signal. The two men ran for the gate in the railings. When the caretaker turned into the saloon-bar entrance they were no more than thirty yards behind. A row of vehicles was parked outside the inn. Last was a dark green delivery wagon. Usher wrenched open the door and slid behind the wheel. As Scott climbed over the seat into the back the wagon was already moving. He braced himself against its lurch, watching through the glass panel in the rear door. Usher spun the truck round the corner and stopped outside the apartment building. He spoke with easy confidence.

" Nobody short of a cop means a thing to us. Remember that! If anyone else comes by, don't give them a second look." He let himself down to the sidewalk.

Scott dragged the iron-tipped planks to the back of the truck. Later they'd be needed to hoist the trolley. He unfastened the loading doors, throwing them wide. He lowered the rubber-tyred trolley into Usher's upstretched arms then the heavy packing-case. Its top was screwed loosely in position. Scott jumped down and shut the doors behind him. By the time he turned, Usher was already at the rear entrance. Scott hauled the trolley up on the kerb. The packing-case rattled in spite of his care. He found himself counting under his breath—as if measuring the seconds were important. The lamp overhead lit the expanse of pavement with startling brilliance. A car whined past on the Embankment, rushing for the traffic signals at the bridge. The jangle of the pub piano was clear. He leaned on the handles of the trolley feeling strangely naked. Already he was imagining the shouts of alarm and running footsteps.

Usher flicked a skeleton key free of its ring. He felt it into the mortise lock with the delicacy of a surgeon. He worked without haste, his blue cashmere coat concealing the deftness of his hands. The door swung inwards. Scott eased the trolley into a darkness that smelt richly of dog. He heard the lock click shut behind him. The feeling of claustrophobia didn't matter—for the moment it was enough to be off the street and safe. It was impossible to know how Craig was feeling. He seemed oblivious to failure. Maybe all professional thieves had the same certainty of success.

Usher's voice came from the blackness ahead. " The light's at the end of the corridor. You've got about twenty feet to go. Take it good and easy. And try to keep the trolley from scraping against the wall."

Scott followed his heart forward. He used both elbows as feelers. He heard Usher unfasten a second door and suddenly he could see. They were in an uncarpeted basement. An arch gave a glimpse of a furnace room—lagged pipes and steam-gauges. A dog's bed lay on the floor inside. On the left was the entrance to the caretaker's flat. Immediately opposite this, an elevator shaft pierced the ceiling.

Scott brushed the green mould and whitewash from his overcoat sleeves and trouser legs. He'd worn the black suit three times in as many years, the last occasion best forgotten. Or maybe the step from funeral to burglary was less indecent than he imagined. It was an offbeat sequence his father would not have found amusing. He scraped conscientiously at the dried horse-dung in the welt of the shoe. Every detail in his behaviour and appearance had been related to his safety since he'd left home that morning. A well-publicised trial disturbed his memory. The report of forensic testimony had been deadly. No more than an unemotional police recital of test-tube contents and microscopic analyses. Yet dust convicted a man with an apparently unshakable alibi. He raised his head to find Usher watching him enigmatically.

His cousin's cheekbones were well-padded, accentuating the hollows between nose and ears. The effect was that of a head sculpted in proportion with makeweight blobs of flesh added as an afterthought. An inch-wide badger streak bisected short black hair, over indifferent blue eyes.

It was as if Usher read his mind. " It's worse if you think about it," he said drily. He jerked back the gate of the tiny elevator. The cage was no more than a metal box designed for the collection of garbage from the upstairs apartments. There was barely room inside for both men and trolley. The noise of the outer gate closing echoed throughout the basement.

Usher pressed the top button. They wedged themselves against the packing-case as the cage started to ascend. The building had no service stairway. Each kitchen door opened directly on to the shaft. The confined space was stifling. Squares of glass set at eye-level marked the passing of each floor. The elevator stopped at the end of its journey, the mechanism releasing the inner swing doors. Usher slid back the outer grille. A simple spring lock barred their way through the white-painted door before them.

Usher slipped a four-inch strip of mica into the gap next the door-jamb. He brought it slowly down till it hit the cup on the far side of the door. He eased it back, clearing the metal flange, then pushed it forward again. The pliable material bent under the steady pressure of his fingers. It curved round the spring-loaded tongue of the lock. As the tongue snapped into its cup, he pushed the door hard with his free hand. The crack in the jamb widened. Something still held the door. He brought the edge of the mica down till it hit the obstruction. Usher twisted his body in the narrow space, his mouth sour and his eyes puzzled.

" Someone's left the bolt on the kitchen door. That's the first time in a month that it's happened. We'll have to go round the front."

Scott was pressed hard against the inner wall of the cage. He noticed the pay-load warning close to his face. His mind was still on what he'd heard of police procedure. It was seven-thirty at night and this was Chelsea—one of the best patrolled areas in the city. From here north to the park, cops were thick on the vine. They lurked behind hoardings, rolled out of driveways in squat black prowl cars. Scotland Yard's advice to householders was categorical and widely disseminated.

6

*Dial 999 if you see anything suspicious. The house you protect may be your own!*

Every maiden aunt and her sister knew the routine these days. What Craig was suggesting made as much sense as surrendering themselves at the nearest police station.

He tried to make his fear sound reasonable. " How the hell do you wheel a trolley along the Embankment?"

"Nobody's wheeling a trolley—I'm going, not you." Usher closed the grille and detached a couple of keys from his ring. His momentary doubt seemed gone. " I've got the front door fitted. I'll be five minutes, no more."

The cage descended to the basement. Scott waited till he heard the back door to the street opened and shut. He pressed the button, sending himself back on his upward journey. Each floor represented a threat. The smell of brewing coffee—the woman's voice raised in inquiry—the snatch of music from a radio. They both had to be crazy taking this sort of chance. The image grew sharp in his mind. This was a service elevator. Someone living in one of these apartments might find reason to use it. There were disposal units down in the basement. He pictured a woman viewing an overfilled garbage can in her kitchen—her decision to empty it—her curiosity hardening to suspicion as the elevator failed to answer her summons.

The cage rattled to a halt at the top floor. He hauled on the outside grille, breaking contact, and switched off the light. A neat trick, he thought hopelessly. Suspended a couple of hundred feet up in the air with no way out.

He bent down, trying to peer underneath the door of the kitchen. The mat inside blocked his view. He put an ear to the current of air, interpreting the whirr of a refrigerator motor, the tick of a clock. He pushed hard with his shoulder, hoping for a miracle. The bolt held firm. It seemed a long time before he heard it withdrawn. He straightened, meeting Usher's impatience defiantly. The trolley rolled in, without sound on the composition flooring. The kitchen was a housewife's dream, as functional and clean as an

7

operating theatre. Chrome and porcelain gleamed everywhere. In the middle of the room a dishwashing machine
was suspended above a circular sink. One wall was lined
with labour-saving gadgets. A deep-freeze unit, infra-red
cooker, an electric stove with as many controls as an airplane cockpit. He found himself comparing the room with
the stone-flagged kitchen at Chestnut Gate. The weekly pot
of linseed for the stables boiling over on the ancient Aga
cooker. The sickly stench of a sheep's-head buried in the
sacks of straw that were the wolfhound's bed.

Usher trod the floor as if it belonged to him. He flipped
the pencilled note standing against the dresser.

*Mrs. Bragg: we shall be late. Please don't disturb us in
the morning. Don't worry about preparing the laundry.
M.C.*

He grinned as though the scribbled message gave the last
touch of authenticity to everything that he had promised.

" What a laugh—don't disturb us."

He led the way into the hall with the familiarity of a
house-guest. As he passed the front door, he thumbed up
the catch, sealing the lock against a key inserted from the
outside. A full-length portrait of a blonde woman hung
over the Provençal chest. Her straight hair was pushed into
a white ermine cap. A matching muff hid her hands. It
was a striking study in white and gold. Scott recognised
the woman he had seen climb into the cab.

Usher patted the painted bosom with gloved fingers.
" And to-night all she had on were the aquamarines. She's
a doll, our Margaret. There isn't a clinker in her collection."

The remark was a reminder that he had moved here
unseen while the owners slept. Sat at a desk, warm in the
sunlight, when the apartment was empty. He had read
their correspondence, catalogued their possessions. In
spite of his cousin's cocksure, theatrical manner, Scott was

impressed. He wheeled the trolley through the door that Usher held open.

The bedroom was apple-green and gilt—the whole of the outer wall a plate-glass window. Far beyond, a lighted bus crawled out of the darkness over Battersea Bridge. The satin cover on the basket-weave bed was turned back. Behind it, photo-montage reproduced the ribaldry of a baroque tapestry. A child's doll lay on one of the pillows, boot-button eyes fixed on the silken canopy that looped from the ceiling. Usher slid back the mirrored front of a clothes closet. A light came on inside.

He jerked his head. "Bring the trolley round this side of the bed. And stay away from the window. They can see you from the street."

He stepped deep into the closet, scattering hangers right and left. He wrenched the clothing from them, using hands and feet like a dog unearthing a bone. The pile of flimsy garments grew on the carpet behind him. The framed picture on the dressing-table fascinated Scott. The man's head drooped slightly, a curl of cigarette smoke obscuring one eye. The other viewed the mounting disorder in the room with incongruous approval. Scott swallowed the thickness in his throat. Something about the picture, the doll on the bed, the bottle of Seltzer ready on the night table, added to his uneasiness. He found himself unable to ignore a lively sense of intrusion.

Usher was hanging, his weight suspended by his hands, on the rail above his head. He kicked one leg free of a trailing gown. He considered the space he had cleared at his feet, speaking almost with affection.

"There it is, Jamie."

A small safe, a couple of feet square, stood on a wooden base. The dial of the combination lock was bright in the bulk of dull steel. The whole created an impression of terrifying impregnability. Usher's hand lingered on the surface like a parlourmaid testing for dust. He embraced the safe with both arms and tugged. The Y-shaped vein

9

grew in his forehead. One edge of the safe tilted. He relinquished his hold, satisfied.

"The makers claim it goes three hundredweight. Get the screws out of the packing-case."

He grabbed an armful of furs and spread them round the pedestal.

Scott wormed the retaining screws from the inch planking. The shake was back in his hands. He tipped the empty crate carefully forward till the open end faced the safe. Then he stepped into the closet with Usher. Both men braced their legs against the back wall. Heads lowered, they heaved against the safe. The mass of metal jerked forward till half its bulk overhung the wooden base. The padded flesh on Usher's cheeks drained of colour. The vein on his forehead was even more distended.

"*Now!*" he gasped.

Under their concerted effort, the safe toppled. It crashed three feet, driving fur into the floor boards. Dust invaded Scott's nostrils. The sweat was running into his eyes. A high-pitched ringing blocked his ears. Usher's exhortation whipped him to fresh strength. Again they upended the safe. This time it did no more than turn its own length, falling squarely on the mink coat. Each man took a sleeve. The end of the safe lifted with their straightening backs. Usher scraped the packing-case forward with one foot. Inch by inch, they repeated the manœuvre till at last the steel box was in its receptacle. Usher wielded the trolley powerfully, ramming its iron-shod nose beneath the crate. His whisper came hoarsely.

"When I take the weight, shove! *Now.*"

He leaned back, eyes shut tight, straining like a spent oarsman. The heavy mass shifted on its fulcrum. Suddenly the tyres sank deep in the pile of the carpet. The trolley was loaded. They worked with new speed, stripping the bed of blankets. These they stuffed into the space between safe and packing-case. Scott refitted the wooden top, drove home the last of the dozen screws. The square box was innocent-looking. Across the cover was a stencilled sign.

KEEP THIS SIDE UP    AGRICULTURAL MACHINERY

The room was a shambles. Smashed glass from the panelled mirrors, ripped clothing, littered the torn carpet. Scott picked the doll from the floor, threw it back on the ransacked bed. He felt an imperative need to leave the enormity they had created.

Usher wiped his neck with a nightdress. His breathing came with difficulty but his light blue eyes were unconcerned.

" I'll give you a hand with the trolley. Try to keep it as low as you can."

They wheeled their load through the hall and into the kitchen. The clock on the dresser showed eleven minutes past eight. The elevator cage was as they had left it, gates open and light out. Scott held the trolley as Usher peered down into the shaft. The rest couldn't miss. Everything had gone the way Craig had said it would. Scott's brain was dull with relief. They'd unload the packing-case at Waterloo. While he found a porter, Craig would dump the wagon. No one would miss the vehicle till Monday. They had allowed themselves half an hour at the railroad station. A fast train pulled out at seven after nine. Once he had paid freight on the case, the scheme was for them to meet in the restaurant car. A meal, a couple of drinks, and the journey would be over. At Basingstoke, British Railways would return the safe. Porters there would remember a crate of farm-machinery loaded into a Land-Rover and nothing more. By the time they reached Chestnut Gate, Parrish would have finished late stables and be back in the village. The house would be empty. Craig claimed six clouts with a sledgehammer would crack the safe open. A hole was already dug on the edge of the gallop. A week's

11

pounding under horses' hooves would hide all sign of the replaced turf.

Usher's voice was warm with appreciation. " Not a sound from below. I told you, the guy runs by clockwork. By the time he gets back we'll be on the train." He snapped the light button and helped ease the trolley on to the platform.

Scott was last in. He thumbed the disc that sent them down. He stood close to the gate, watching the top floor disappear. The iron framework outside seemed to climb, leaving them stationary. Door after door flashed by while overhead the cable screamed on its pulley. The speed of their descent increased, rattling the cage in its guides. Suddenly Usher hurled himself away from the shifting trolley. His mouth opened in a soundless yell. Both men bent double, protecting their heads with their arms. For a moment it seemed as if the elevator would halt at the basement floor. High in the shaft, the stop-mechanism shuddered, seeking to function. Then a cog tore loose. The cage plummeted the last few feet into the inspection pit. The lights went out.

A smothering weight was pinning Scott to the floor. He fought it blindly. A gloved hand covered his nose and lips, shutting off his breath. He lay completely still then felt Usher roll away. The same hand hauled him to his feet. He steadied himself against the packing-case, looking out into darkness.

The acceptance was bitter—it was of a piece with the rest. A failure as useless and ignominious as the struggle to run indifferent horses into the winner's frame. Prison would merely resolve his problems more quickly. The bank would move in on Chestnut Gate. There'd probably be an auction. Good luck to those who attended it. Nothing he owned was worth risking a back axle to investigate. Maybe Parrish would take Sam. To anyone else, a full-grown wolfhound would be about as welcome as a baboon. Less, probably—Sam ate meat.

Usher's snarl sliced through the wave of self-pity.

"Kick the gates open, for Chrissakes!"

Scott leaned back till his shoulders were against his cousin's chest. He lifted a knee, driving his foot as hard as he could against the divided doors. They swung outwards for no more than inches. Usher's impetus added force to Scott's next effort. The doors yawed again. The pit wall prevented them from opening fully. Usher managed to scramble by. He groped in the filth on the ground, coming up with a scrap of metal. With it he wedged one side of the door. A wad of paper held the other at the limit of its swing. They were still trapped at ground level by concrete and steel. But the space gained above their heads was enough to allow passage of a man's head and shoulders.

Usher stood on the packing-case. He reached up, caught the framework of the shaft, the lower half of his body dangling. He chinned himself slowly, kicked back and landed on top of the elevator cage. Scott followed. They crouched in the shadow thrown by the girders. Left and right were the guide-rails, thick with noisome grease. The cable above was a tenuous link with the pent-house, two hundred feet away. It still hummed on a faint, deep note —like a 'cello string struck by accident. Only the trellis grille was between them and the hall in front of the caretaker's apartment. Usher tried its handle. The gate slid an inch on its latch to hold firm on the raised flange. Usher's instruction was tense.

"Give me the screwdriver."

Scott was searching his pockets as the door opened four floors up. The elevator shaft was suddenly illuminated. A man's voice called in alarm. The beam of a flashlight searched the darkness.

Usher took the screwdriver. "Don't look up!" he warned. He jammed the tool under the flange. It snapped, the broken end pinging into the well below. He rammed the shortened stub in still farther. The beam of light

13

settled on top of the cage. A man's voice echoed down the shaft.

"Is that you, Harris? Harris—are you all right?"

Usher's body tightened with strain. "The bottom—lift the bottom."

Head between his knees, Scott obeyed. The long, flat muscles in his back were agony. His legs wavered. Suddenly the gate gave with a loud report then concertinaed on its own length. He pitched forward into the hallway, falling on outstretched hands. There was no further sound from the floor above. No more than the faintest reverberation that followed them down the corridor. Usher was already fumbling with the first door. He spat his words as if in speaking he might destroy all pursuit.

"We've got about three minutes. Let's go."

They ran the length of the passage blindly. The street door slammed against the wall as they burst through it and into the wagon. The starter hit first time. Usher rammed into bottom gear, gunning the vehicle across the street. They were twenty yards on and cornering the Embankment when a group of people ran from the front of the building. Scott leaned his head against cool metal. He shut his eyes, oblivious to everything save the sound of the motor. When at last he opened them, the wagon was stationary.

He stared at the scene through the windshield. It had become essential to know precisely where he was. The stream of traffic ahead jockeyed its way into Sloane Square. The buses like galleons in a swarm of rowboats, bullied their way north. Fifty yards away, the snowflakes dropped hesitantly on the deserted concourse. The fountain in the centre of the square played in a floodlit haze to deserted benches. Nearer at hand, a few pedestrians sheltered in the doorway opposite the bus-stop.

A match flared beside him. Usher's face bent into the flame. He drew hard on his cigarette, his eyes assessing.

"Are you O.K., Jamie?"

Scott worked a Gauloise from the bottom of the pack.

He had no idea how he was supposed to feel and didn't care. He needed his head examined, that's all he knew.

"I'm O.K.," he said shortly. "I just want to get the hell out of here as fast as I can."

Usher sped a stream of smoke through pursed lips.

"If you flip now, you're gone. Try to be rational. The cab rank's empty. We'll take the first one that comes along. We're safe enough until then. Nobody got our number."

They were parked on the short street at the side of Sloane Square station. Thirty yards away, people were hurrying into the entrance.

"You do what you like," Scott said violently. "I'm taking the subway."

Usher caught him half-way to the sidewalk, pulling him back in his seat. The younger man leant across and closed the door.

"Suit yourself. But take some of that crap off your clothes unless you want to be pulled in as a tramp."

He lit the dashboard, screwing the driving mirror so that the other could see.

Scott looked up cautiously—as if the drama of events should have left more than just a grease-streaked cheek, a sleeve snagged by torn metal. He did his best with his handkerchief, balled it and stuffed it deep in a pocket. His voice was flat and uncompromising.

"Three thousand pounds apiece. An hour's work and no kickback. Brother, when am I going to learn?"

Usher busied himself with his own repairs. Not till he was done did he answer.

"You're making it sound as though you've done me a favour. Let me ask you one thing, Jamie. Do you really think I needed you to-night?"

The injustice of the question fired Scott to anger. "If you didn't, you sure made it sound plausible. What was it —charity?"

Usher hitched a shoulder. "Maybe my memory's longer than yours. And kinder. I always figured you to be on my

15

side—me on yours. Is that what you call being charitable?"

Something in the other's tone checked Scott's hostility. He answered carefully. "If the letters are still worrying you, we've done that bit to death. I've already told you—the last news I had about you was three years ago at the funeral. The family had a great time explaining exactly why you couldn't be there. You said you wrote me from jail. I never had a single letter."

Usher lowered the window and dropped his butt to the street.

"You wouldn't be here if I didn't believe that," he said simply. "I'm trying to explain why you *are* here. How about the pitch you gave me in Canada House?"

Scott's own cigarette was suddenly without flavour. The scene was too fresh and vivid to forget. The first awkward encounter outside the passport renewal office. Craig's face stony with accusation. As though in Scott he confronted the embodiment of a hostile and critical family. The whispered conversation across a table in the Reading Room. Finally, the little restaurant where they'd eaten, the first time together in five years.

He chose his words. "I never gave you a pitch in my life, Craig. You asked how things were with me. I told you."

Usher drove himself like a man who needed a fuller explanation. "You told me! How did you expect *me* to help? You know the trust fund went ten years ago. And you know how I've lived since."

Scott smoothed the thin doeskin over his knuckles. He was being shoved against a wall—forced into self-analysis. Secretly, he supposed, he'd been hoping to latch on to Craig's reputation for ingenuity. It was a legend in the family—you don't worry about Craig, he always falls on somebody else's feet. Certainly he'd offered a solution and Scott hadn't balked at the conditions.

"What's the use," he said finally. "We blew it to-night

and that's that. I'd like to think I'm no worse off than I was two hours ago. But I'm not sure."

Usher shrugged himself upright, self-critical.

"You're right. What happened back there was my fault —not yours. I checked everything but the pay-load. But at least we're still in circulation."

Without seeing the expression on the other's face, Scott recognised the talent for retrieving good from bad. Nothing Craig ever did was without some involved virtue. Scott found his cousin's last words oddly disquieting. *In circulation.* Just a few hours ago, he'd belonged with the people hurrying into the subway. Jail was no more than a place that you read about. It had no real dimensions—not even when Craig had gladdened the hearts of most of the family by landing there. To-night, Scott found himself appreciative of the impermanence of freedom for the first time in his life. His mind went back to the elevator shaft, the flashlight playing on his shoulders. A point square in the centre of his back seemed to burn with the memory.

Usher's outburst took him by surprise. "I tell you I could have had a pro with me to-night. Someone who'd have done his job and kept his mouth shut afterwards. Jesus God, Jamie—we're both still in trouble. Nobody's going to pin a medal on you because you've beaten a police alarm. You're still in hock to the bank—I still need to eat. Don't you understand that—nothing's changed!"

Scott somehow kept his voice steady. "I'll tell you what I understand. The law of averages. I'm not going to buck it twice. There's something else—maybe you're not as good at this lark as everyone thinks you are."

Chance sent a couple of cabs to the rank across the square. Usher turned, taking a last look in the back of the wagon. He closed the partition. His smile was without malice.

"You always had a fresh mouth. Let's move. Is it all right with you if I still come down to your place? After to-night's performance, I feel like air."

17

There was something disarming in the suggestion—a reminder of a time long since gone. A couple of kids burnt
brown by the August sun, swatting mosquitoes as they
hauled the canoe from the white-sand beach into the
shelter of the pines. The school ice-rink—the last frozen
second as he steadied the puck to drive it into the net. And
behind the mesh, Craig with a butch haircut and knicker-
bockers, purple-faced with excitement.

Scott pulled the gloves from his fingers. He made up his
mind to dump them in the first refuse bin that he saw. He
was sick of everything that they stood for. His grin was
wry.

"O.K. But air's about all that you'll get. Ain't nothing
else left on this farm."

: :                    : :

The down-train clattered over the points into Basingstoke
Station. The public-address system greeted its arrival in a
flat Hampshire accent. The litany of towns and times
droned on. Scott leaned from the open window. The news-
stand was boarded up for the night. Three soldiers slept on
the bench beside it, held upright by their kitbags. A pair of
porters trotted after the first-class carriages. The ticket collector was talking to a woman with a child at the exit. For
this hour, the station seemed normal enough.

He unlatched the door. The two men climbed out, the
only alighting passengers. Usher's white-streaked hair was
wet with water. He wore his dark-blue overcoat like a
cloak, the torn sleeve pulled through its armhole and hidden. He was a step in front of Scott as they walked along
the platform. Suddenly he came to an abrupt halt, blocking the other's way. He went through the motions of con-
sulting a train schedule, his lips barely moving.

"Is that cop always there?"

The uniformed policeman stood beyond the barrier. The
face under the domed helmet was familiar and, for Scott,
suddenly sinister. He wet his bottom lip with the end of his
tongue and swallowed.

"For drunks and deserters. He's harmless."

Usher moved on again, smiling faintly. Only now he was behind as Scott went through the barrier—the featured player deferring to the star. Scott surrendered the tickets. The mechanics were bound by protocol that went back six months. A blind tip on a horse had started it. Success had left the collector convinced of Scott's omniscience. The Canadian cut short the hoarsely secret inquiry.

"I don't know a thing, Jim. Maybe next week."

He was half-way across the booking hall when he realised that he was walking alone. He looked back to see Usher standing in front of the Departure Board. Scott watched with irritation as his cousin completed the pointless perusal, nodded good night to the policeman and made his way outside.

A single-decker bus was turning in the station yard. Inside, a bunch of beer-happy youths were heckling the driver. The Land-Rover was parked by one of the loading bays at the end of the freight depot. It was dark there save for a thin shaft of light from the handler's office. Scott pushed home the ignition key. The motor kicked, pistons slapping into rhythm.

His back and legs still ached. Above all, he was disturbed by Usher's flamboyance. At a time like this, display seemed lunatic. He neither favoured nor understood the other man's need of it. He tried to put the feeling into words.

"Just in case it's of interest—that cop spent seven years in the navy. He'd knock a pheasant out of the sky before you saw it and he's read Shakespeare. Who the hell do you think you're impressing with that hamming?"

Usher slipped both arms into his overcoat. "It was for me, not him. Unless you understand what I'm trying to say, you'll never take a penny from a blind man without rattling the cup."

Scott swung the Land-Rover into the station approach. They rolled out into the Saturday night bustle of a country town. Past the emptying cinemas, the teenagers lounging in the garish light outside a fish-and-chip parlour. On by belated window-shoppers caught by an assault on their purse and credulity. Finally, the last pub sign glowed at the end of town—an outpost against encroaching loneliness.

The freshening wind had chased the cloud, revealing a cold moon pasted against an endless sky. The snowfall had stopped. In spite of its age, the motor was reliable. They drove fast behind dimmed headlights. Beyond the hedgerows stretched the pale gold of stubbled fields, glistening with moisture. The road narrowed, cutting west, parallel to the A30. A solid white line unwound on the macadamed surface, dragging the speeding vehicle past cottages spiked with television aerials. At Oakley, Scott forked right in the direction of Hannington. Now the countryside began to billow into hills lost in the darkness. A few miles on, he eased his foot on the accelerator. They rounded a bend, passing a sawmill, clean and ghostly in the moonlight. A pretentious-looking inn sprawled at the end of the short village street. The style was Roadhouse Tudor. Fake beams set in plaster, leaded mullions and swinging coach-lanterns. Half a dozen cars were still parked on the concrete lot.

Usher twisted his head towards the sound of music. "Want to bet I don't call the score on that one? They're very high on tone and the landlord calls you 'old boy.' His wife wears dresses cut to display her knockers. They know all about cold beer and mix martinis half-and-half."

In spite of himself, Scott laughed. The long silence had softened his mood. Beyond the austere outline of church and vicarage was home.

"Fair enough. The landlord's a piss-elegant major who's his own best customer. A couple of years ago, that place was a decent village pub. You can see what they've done to it. I only go there when I'm sick of my own drink."

He wheeled past the stone water-trough, slowing for the blind turn to Chestnut Gate. The light was still on downstairs in Parrish's cottage. Son and mother, they'd be sitting there, stone-deaf without their hearing aids, communicating by signs. The old woman was eighty, with all the asperity of her age and affliction. Every morning, when he went home to breakfast, Parrish carried her downstairs. There she sat the long day, wrapped in shawls, summer and winter. A shaving mirror tilted outside the window gave her a clear view of the road. The village children eyed it longingly— none dared to heave a rock. The polished square of glass drove courting couples to the neighbouring lanes, banished boisterous teenagers to the pub parking lot, the waste behind the sawmill.

The lane skirted the trees at the back of the vicarage garden. Headlights picked out a painted sign poking over a white gate.

### SLOW FOR HORSES

Scott jumped out. He pushed back the gate and hooked it against the bank of rhododendrons. Rooks cawed in the uppermost darkness of the oak trees behind him. The deep baying of a wolfhound came from the lighted stableyard a quarter mile away.

The Land-Rover jolted up the incline, springs banging as its wheels hit the bottoms of the chuckholes. The paved stableyard was the size of a tennis-court, enclosed on three sides. On one, the front had been knocked out of a cow-byre, the space behind converted to loose-boxes. Four heads craned over the half-doors, ears pricked at the sound of the motor. The back of an L-shaped farmhouse completed the square. Scott ran the Land-Rover under a barn, next to a two-horse trailer. He jumped out. The brindled hound leaped at him, tail lashing. It rose on its hind legs, the size of a calf, front paws landing on Scott's shoulders. He staggered under the impact, six inches of tongue slobbering his ear. He caught the dog beneath the armpits and stepped back.

21

"Christ!" said Usher with feeling. "The original Hound of the Baskervilles!" He stood stockstill while the animal nosed the cuffs of his trousers.

Scott's snapping fingers sent the hound into a ludicrous lumbering hop. "I wouldn't call Sam bright. But he's kind. I've seen him mad twice. The relief postman and some smart sonofabitch collie. He didn't break the skin on either occasion."

He put his hand into gentle jaws, half-leading, half-led, across the yard to the loose-boxes. He drew the top bolt and stepped inside. The chestnut gelding whipped round, wide nostrils splayed. Scott straightened the twisted night-rug, his voice soothing. He ran his fingers over a joint—feeling for heat—pulled a strand of hay from the net. It was still sweet and heady from last year's sun.

Conscious of Usher's inspection, he looked up. His cousin was leaning against the whitewash, twirling a straw in his mouth. He spoke easily and pleasantly.

"You surprise me, Jamie. I never realised just how seriously you took all this."

Scott turned away, suspicious of sarcasm. There was no accepted formula for explaining that this was what he lived for.

"It suits me," he said shortly.

Usher kicked through the bedding to measure himself against the restive chestnut's withers.

"Must go sixteen hands. How's he bred?"

The facile professionalism of the inquiry, the straw whirling in Usher's mouth, riled Scott. They were being given Usher The Horseman just as earlier it had been Usher The Burglar.

"Either put that cigarette out," Scott said shortly, "or take it into the yard." He turned his back deliberately, finding something to do until he heard the bottom half of the door close. He checked each box, quitting the last with a reminder that he must have Parrish change the feed-tub in the mare's stable. Usher was across the yard, talking to the hound. They followed Scott into the dressed-leather smell of the saddle room. He chalked a message on Parrish's slate and propped it on a locker.

" I'll show you the house."

Usher was leafing through the racing calendar on the wall. The naked bulb hanging from the ceiling afforded light for what came next—a complete survey of the room. Then he smiled—a disclaimer of anything but friendly comment.

" You know something, Jamie—you're on the defensive about everything you own. Everything you've done. I'm not trying to give you a hard time, believe me. It's a fact."

Scott grinned shamefacedly. " And the man's looking for fresh air! Let's say life isn't easy at the moment."

" Was it ever easy?" asked Usher. The bridle chinked softly in his hand. He swung it a couple of times in the air then replaced it on its hook. His expression was thoughtful.

" Since I'm here, how about a ride? I'd like that."

Scott straddled the stool, his astonishment frank. " The crazy bit is that you mean it. These animals aren't park hacks, Craig. You wouldn't hold one side of any of them."

Usher crossed the room, hazy blue eyes challenging. He stretched out a leg for Scott's inspection. " Feel," he invited.

Scott poked the inside of the thigh. The riding muscle was flat and hard. He shrugged.

" A thoroughbred's a different proposition."

Usher found the hound's neck with sensitive fingers. The animal leaned its ruff into the pressure.

" Who taught who to jump fences?" he asked quietly.

Scott rejected the memory. " That's going back twenty years. I've got enough on my mind at the moment without you upstairs nursing a smashed arm."

" Balls," said Usher. " I'm too valuable a property to bust up that easily."

Scott caught the dog's mesh collar. He was oddly hesi-

23

tant. He found another reason for denial. " I don't work them Sundays."

Usher was still determined. " You will this Sunday. As a favour, Jamie." He walked out to the yard as though the matter were settled.

Scott turned the lock on the saddle room. The gallop was a mile-and-a-half long. Craig would be less sure of himself at the end of it. The thought gave pleasure.

" You've got yourself a ride. The kitchen door's straight ahead."

A hundred and twenty years had sagged the roof of the low building. A deep carpet of ivy covered the fieldstone walls, untrimmed except round the casement windows. In the clear moonlight, the farmhouse was an integral part of the hillside. A shelter rather than a setting. Inside was an impression of warmth and shabbiness. Fibre matting insulated the flagged kitchen floor. Someone had set the clean scrubbed table for a solitary meal. A haphazard collection of race-badges, cups and keys hung from hooks on the old-fashioned dresser. Copies of the *Sporting Life* were stacked on top of a bread-bin. A stained hunting mac was drying near the range cooker.

Scott drew the sitting-room curtains. He kicked the logs in the open fireplace. The blaze reflected on black, polished floorboards. The brass tub was filled with sawn apple-billets, Parrish's last undemanded chore. Scott found himself looking at the room with the eye of a stranger. Unmatched armchairs, their seats and backs shaped into comfortable hollows—a round useless table and one decent standard lamp. The rugs were still good and every book on the white shelves had been read.

Craig was wrong. His life needed no defence—just a continuance. The wolfhound sprawled on the mat in front of the fire. Usher kicked off his shoes and used the dog's back as a rest for his feet. He locked both hands behind his neck, watching Scott splash soda into two glasses of whisky. He tasted his drink and put it on the floor beside him.

"I suppose there must be people like you all over England. Training a few horses under permit. With a difference, though. They've either got money or they make it."

Scott lowered himself into the vacant chair. The night's near-disaster still worried its way into his thinking. He had a perverse and persistent wish to talk about it. An urge to relive his escape. He envied Usher's ability to pull a blind on the spectacle.

"What's wrong about making money?" he asked simply.

Usher ran his instep the length of the hound's backbone. "About making money, nothing. But you don't. Handled properly, a place like this could provide a legitimate living."

Scott laughed openly. "Since when did you qualify as a financial expert? It took you fourteen months to run a hundred thousand dollar trust fund into the ground. I wouldn't say your record since has been brilliant."

The firelight tinged Usher's face copper. He made the old flat-handed gesture of defeat.

"I learnt the hard way. I've never had enough money at any one time over these past eight years—otherwise you'd have a neighbour."

Scott emptied his glass. Craig had always been a master of the dramatic volte-face—the quick change of front that landed him squarely on your side of the argument. The manœuvre was even more baffling if you understood that in both instances he was sincere.

Scott was forbearing. "I'm way ahead of you. O.K. You're installed in your six-bedroomed manor-house. You've got a pedigree herd of Jerseys and a farm bailiff. Then what?"

Usher's mouth was serious. "You're wrong," he corrected—"I've got a place just like this. And a contented bank manager. Every time I clipped a dividend coupon I'd buy a horse. Then I'd be racing for pleasure—not to pay my feed bills."

A log collapsed in the grate. The hound's great head lifted, nose twitching, amber eyes intent on the brightening flame. Scott yawned frankly.

"You ought to put that on paper. A magazine like *Country Life* might buy it. The trouble is, Craig, you're like me—broke flatter than a sausage skin. You want another drink?"

He carried the two glasses over to the table and shook life into the tired siphon.

Usher put his feet on the floor and found his shoes. He seemed determined that Scott should take him seriously.

"Suppose I told you that within a month I'll have my hands on thirty thousand quid—possibly more."

The bottle wavered in Scott's hand. He mopped the liquid he had spilled on the table, suddenly apprehensive.

"You couldn't hock a statement like that for a fiver in this house."

"Maybe not." Usher's voice was harsh as if he must offset any return to sentimentality. "We grew up together, Jamie. I used to think you were nine feet tall. You're the only person I never lied to, goddamnit. Do you accept that?"

Instinct told Scott that the question was loaded. He bent over the logs, pushing a spill of paper into the embers. He found a cigarette in the box on the mantel. Loaded or not, he had to answer honestly.

"I don't think you'd lie to me, no."

Usher stood up in turn. He leaned his forehead against the wall, looking down into the fireplace.

"There's a lot of crap taken for granted about thieves. I'll give you facts. A thief's imagination takes him from one score to the next—no further. I don't care how good the guy is. When he sits around the table, counting the take, he's got just one idea. How to get rid of it. It's part of jailhouse philosophy. He's not worrying about profit margins—picket lines—or whether Aunt Tillie's milking the cash register. When the money's gone, there's always another mug to beat. He thinks the laws of averages is just another joke on the Statute Book. I went along with the gag for six years, Jamie. That's the time it took to understand one simple proposition. In my business you have to operate from strength. Hit and hit again and then out. That's what I'm doing now."

Scott lowered himself to the arm of a chair. This was the old Craig, popping at you from the bushes. In a minute, he'd break cover, yelling to make sure you knew he was there.

"Run it up the flagpole and see who salutes—not me."

Usher's back straightened. He started to pace the room from wall to wall. The sarcasm he ignored.

"Your father had me pegged. He said 'The only thing about Craig that isn't idle is his brain.' He was right, Jamie. He might have added that I'm persistent. I don't like jail. I don't intend going back there. What would you know about being broke! You eat what you like—if you want a case of Scotch, you buy it. I've lived for four months on canned beans and milk—till the stuff runs out of my ears. You know why? Because for four months I've been nursing two coups for the right moment. To-night was meant to be the first. I won't miss with the other. You can be part of it."

Scott wound his fingers into the hound's ruff and led him into the kitchen. He riddled the stove, emptied a scuttle of coal into the range. He set the alarm for six-thirty and went back to the sitting-room.

"If you still want that ride, we'd better get some rest. I'll show you your room. You'll find pyjamas in the airing cupboard—toothbrushes in the bathroom."

Usher placed the screen in front of the fire, his face impassive. "Am I to take it you've retired—that once is enough? You must be crazy."

Scott's shoulders filled the doorway. "What's so crazy about staying out of jail?"

Usher balanced the question in two hands before throwing it away. "What'll you do—pray or sit on your arse till the bank pulls the chair from under you?"

Scott was unmoved. "You may not like this, Craig, but I'll still be here when you're getting another number sewn on your sleeve. This time you'll be sure where you can send your letters. And this time, they'll be answered."

Usher shook his head slowly. "Nine feet tall, did I say? You're a long way short of that. Let's hit the sack." He was whistling softly as he climbed the stairs.

Scott heard the whistle long after he had finished in the bathroom. He shut his door against its toneless persistence. Craig would need jodhpurs and boots, a sweater, in the morning. He laid a spare kit on the bottom of his bed and put out the light. For a while, he stood at the open window, looking down at the stableyard brilliant under the moon. He heard a horse shift, thudding its hind quarters against the partition. A barn cat streaked from the straw rick, hunting a mouse beneath the trailer. He was filled with a sense of loneliness. He'd talked a great last-ditch stand downstairs. The truth was, wherever he'd be at the end of the month, it wouldn't be here. Craig knew only the half of it. The bank had held the deeds to Chestnut Gate for over three years. They knew to a nickel how far to stretch an overdraft. There'd be enough money to eat—to pay Parrish's wages—for another three weeks, maybe. Then they'd force the sale. It wasn't the bank, though, that would finally finish him. The Internal Revenue was on his back. Dorfman had spelled it out in simple language. Either Scott paid his tax arrears or he'd be made bankrupt. Sixteen hundred pounds before the thirtieth of the month. The lawyer had taken time out to explain the alternative. Once the court had made the order, a bankrupt owned nothing but his clothes and the tools of his trade. What the bank didn't claim would belong to the Official Receiver or vice versa. Craig was wrong. He knew all about being broke. He stretched between cold sheets, burying Dorfman's pessimism deep in the pillow.

# JAMES SCOTT

SUNDAY

The chestnut's jaws snaked round, ears flattening as Scott tightened the girth. He grabbed the animal's muzzle above the nostrils. A hind leg lashed token defiance. He led the horse out to the yard, held its head as Usher swung into the saddle. Usher sat easily, the borrowed sweater bagging round his neck. He shortened his stirrup leathers and jogged round the yard. He pulled up, looking down at Scott.

"What about a bat?"

The rangy bay swung in a tight circle, feeling Scott's weight in the saddle. He patted the muscled neck.

"You'll have enough to do without a whip. You're riding too short as it is. If that animal puts in a buck, you'll land in the next county."

Usher grinned. "Go peddle your papers," he said distinctly. He pulled down his cap and turned his mount in behind Scott's.

They trotted in Indian file, up a lane overgrown with briar, into the grey stillness of the December morning. Moss deadened the sound of the horses' hooves. They rode in a silence unbroken save for the creaking of leather. Scott rose to the bay's awkward trot. It had been before six when he heard his cousin moving in the kitchen. He'd dragged himself from bed, padding down the stairs in bare feet to find the stove replenished and tea made. Usher was sitting in the kitchen arm-chair, eyes closed, the dog's head resting in his lap. Scott was somehow embarrassed— like a house-guest who blunders into the wrong room. He turned his back, clattering the half-pint mugs against the tea-pot. He avoided Sam's butted greeting. Usher opened his eyes slowly. His mouth set in a wry curve as if he were conscious of being detected in a display that he deprecated.

" I've been up an hour. The bed was too soft and everything too quiet. The windows didn't even rattle."

Scott shoved the bowl of sugar across the table. Caught offguard in that split second, Usher's face had shown a contentment beyond pretence. As though he were really part of the house and the life lived there. The thought was both welcome and disturbing. For the next hour, neither man had ventured beyond generalities.

A gate barred the end of the lane. Scott turned the bay broadside on, bent down and freed the latch. He held the gate wide for Usher. The stretch of turf ahead followed the flattened ridge of the hill. A mile-and-a-half away, it dropped into a spinney. Post-and-rail fencing bounded the thirty-yard-wide gallop. Tilled fields sloped into hollows on each side. Far behind the trees was the village. The breeze carried the rushed, uneven tolling of the church bell.

Usher reined in the chestnut at the first painted marker. He had pulled his cap even lower, imprisoning his ears. He nodded across at the ploughland.

" Is that yours?"

Scott shifted his mount out of kicking distance. He shortened his grip on the reins, made a bridge in them and drove his heels home in the irons.

" Just what you see between the rails—that and the back paddock. Jump off after me and stay there. This isn't a race. That horse knows more about it than you do. And sit still. Don't go charging all over the place."

He clicked the bay into a hack canter. Twenty seconds later, he shifted the centre of balance, his hands creeping up the bay's neck. The horse stretched into a steady, half-speed gallop. Scott lowered his face into the sudden rush of wind. As he passed the six furlong marker, he heard the chestnut coming fast on his inside. For a moment he thought the animal was loose. Then he saw Usher, bent almost double, scrubbing the gelding into top speed. Before Scott could drive his mount up in its bit the chestnut was four lengths ahead.

The wind drove Scott's shout back in his throat. The crazy bastard wouldn't be able to stop. All that lay between the end of the track and the trees was a thin screen of planking. At thirty miles an hour, a horse would go through it like a hot fly through butter. Whether either of them lived afterwards was something again. The mile post flicked by. The bay's stride lengthened. Any moment, he'd have to start pulling up himself. He shouted a second time, uselessly. Then the chestnut seemed to be coming back to him. Another hundred yards and it broke gait. Its neck curved to Usher's steady leverage. By the time Scott cantered up, Usher had dropped his hands and was walking his mount in a circle. He held the reins loosely as the chestnut shook itself like a wet dog. He let out a couple of holes in his girth and stuck a cigarette in his mouth. For a man out of practice it was an impressive performance.

Scott's voice was shaking. " I said stay behind, didn't I ! Why do you always have to be a wise guy?"

Usher's friendly slap sent the chestnut dancing. He pushed up his cap, his expression innocent.

" I thought you were waving me on. What *were* you doing, catching flies?"

The absurdity left Scott helpless. He was unable to keep from answering the other's grin.

" That sort of crack could get you a fat lip. All right—let's have it—where in hell *have* you been riding?"

Usher was almost smug. It seemed the moment he had been waiting for.

" Ah that ! I'll tell you. A little number called Caroline Woodall. She's got a mother down in Kent who keeps a couple of point-to-pointers. I've been spending the odd week-end down there."

Something in his cousin's tone made Scott curious.

"Your taste in women must have changed," he said suspiciously. "It doesn't sound like anyone I ever saw you with. There must be an angle."

Usher's cigarette smoke hung in the cold air. He pitched away the butt.

"You're a cynic, that's your trouble, Jamie. She's got nothing except the key to thirty thousand quid."

He reined alongside, settled the chestnut to a walk. They started back up the gallop. It was as much as he would say all the way back to the stables.

They unsaddled in pale sunlight. Already the yard had been swept and hosed. The wolfhound was dozing on a mat outside the kitchen door. Scott carried the gear into the saddle room. The Sunday papers were where Parrish had left them. Scott searched the damp pages, fingers clumsy with haste. Nowhere was there any mention of an attempted robbery in Chelsea. He shut his ears against the now frantic tolling of the church bell. The omission was ominous. A crated safe at the bottom of an elevator shaft must be news. The police would have been at the building within minutes. It had to be some sort of trick. He heard the boards creak outside and tried to stuff the newspapers into his windbreaker pocket. He was too late.

Usher ran a hand over his magpie scalp. His smile was indulgent.

"What did you expect—your picture on the front page? I keep telling you—the cops have everything but a crystal ball."

Scott pushed by without answering. The door to the first loose-box was open. Inside, a short spare man of sixty was hissing as he wielded a straw wisp of the chestnut's polished quarters. A deaf-aid lead dangled from Parrish's ear. He wore old-fashioned gaiters. Weather had buffed the skin on his face and neck to a high, glazed finish. He ducked his head at Scott's inquiry, the movement graphic with disapproval.

Scott was patient. He might have guessed that the gallop

32

wouldn't be popular with the groom. Parrish's God was a countryman with stern requirements of His faithful. A bearded Victorian God, barely tolerant of electricity. Parrish laboured, honoured and did his best to keep holy the seventh day. For him, beasts of burden included thoroughbred horses, Sundays they rested.

Scott pitched his voice on a common wave length. "Were there any phone calls for me yesterday?" There was a phone extension in the saddle room. The outsize bell on the yard wall rang loud enough for Parrish to hear. The groom rugged the gelding and took off its head collar.

"The butcher. You were supposed to call for the dog-meat. I done it."

The flat Hampshire drawl held no grudge—merely a reminder that whoever forgot the animals it wouldn't be Parrish. His day was only complete when his work was done. Expediency governed the hours he put in. He toiled slowly and quietly, achieving order and comfort where two men half his age must have failed. His loyalty was complete but it was to house and stables rather than to their owner.

Scott bawled his thanks. "I'm glad you thought of it. I was late back."

Parrish's foot dragged bedding to block any draught and shut the half-door. He wheeled his bicycle from the feed room. Like everything else connected with him, the machine was spotless and cared for. It was painted an incongruous vermilion and the raked handlebars pitched his body forward at a daring angle. He rose on the pedals, spry as a jay.

"Mother seen you," he said shortly.

The heat in the kitchen was stifling. Scott turned back the range regulator and opened a window. He slapped a torpid wasp from the window sill and set about preparing breakfast with the unthinking precision of years of practice. The overflow pipe spilled into the yard as Usher wallowed in the bath upstairs. He came down wearing his own slacks, shaved and relaxed. The top half of his body was bulky in an old tweed jacket of Scott's. He sniffed the coffee appreciatively. They ate as men do when alone, the newspapers spread in front of them. An arm of winter sunlight stretched across the kitchen, invading the angle in the whitewashed walls where the dog slept. Usher shaded his eyes. He spoke like a man with few wants unsatisfied.

"This is like old times, Jamie—up at the lake. Remember the job they'd have to get us back to the Valley?"

Scott imprisoned the strong black tobacco deep in his lungs. He remembered every sight, sound and smell. The cedar-built camp, shuttered for the winter months. The path through spruce and maple, deep in red-gold leaves and dotted with deer dung. The rickety landing-stage at the end of the trail, pushing out into the cold green water. His father had stood erect in the bobbing motor boat, calling their names. The shout echoed in the trees where they lay, postponing the sadness of leaving. As his father's summons persisted, he and Craig had shouldered the burlap bags and walked reluctantly to the waiting boat. Heedless of driving spray, they'd watched the white crescent of beach disappear from sight. At sixteen, next summer was a lifetime away.

He had a sudden bitter sense of loss that went with the memory. He piled the dirty plates in the sink, aiming a jet of hot water at the moulded bacon grease. The hell with it —he was too old to start all over again. Usher lounged against the window looking at the sky. He was obviously done with teenage memories.

"I've got an ache in my left ankle that says snow. I thought I'd take a walk. You want to come?"

Scott shook his head, turning away so that the other would not read his expression.

"I've got things to take care of. Give Sam a run. Try the paddock back of the barn. You might put up a hare. Don't worry about the hound. He knows the country."

He stood behind the sitting-room curtains till he saw

Usher and the dog climb above the skyline. He followed them out to the yard. A shovel was strapped on the flat hood of the Land-Rover. He put the vehicle in reverse and turned into the lane leading up to the gallops. A chalky patch gaped in the turf to one side of the starting marker. This was the hole that was meant to have buried the safe. He'd dug it at night with the furtiveness of someone preparing a grave—starting guiltily when a steer coughed in the darkness. Later he had burnished the blade of the shovel to Parrish's own standard of perfection and replaced it.

Now he started spading in the light soil. In a sense, it was the end of a chapter. He wanted no one to see him close it. The sun lost its strength suddenly, darkening straw-littered fields. Down in the hollow, the grey tower of the Norman church poked from a huddle of houses. He trod the turf roughly back in position and drove back to the yard.

There was enough hot water for a second bath. When he was done, he carried his clothes to the kitchen, padding naked over warm fibre-matting. He draped the crumpled silk shirt on a board and ran a steam-iron across the collar, front and cuffs. Dark brown shoes matched the herring-bone suit. He dressed and sat in the cane chair, his mind still striving helplessly with figures.

It was gone noon when the door to the yard shook under the weight of the wolfhound's paws. The animal came into the kitchen, thrashing its tail benevolently. Scott's wrist was caught in kind jaws. He pulled himself free and slapped the dog to its bed.

Wind and exercise had whipped a semblance of well-being into Usher's cheeks. His grin was as vast as the hound's.

" I guess even the hares know it's Sunday. All we found was one old dog-badger. Dead."

He whistled approval of Scott's attire. Scott found his cousin's manner increasingly difficult to take. Like all

Craig's productions, the role demanded more of the audience than the performer.

"There's nothing here to eat for lunch," Scott said briefly. "We'll have to go to the pub."

Usher supported himself against the wall, using a table-knife to scrape the caked mud from his shoes.

"Suits me. Tell me something, Jamie. How much are you into the bank for?"

Scott raised his shoulders. For the last year or so, the red digits had been stencilled on his mind. As fine and clear as they came off the electric typewriter. Said aloud, the sum had no relation to reality.

"Four thousand, five hundred pounds."

Usher tossed the knife into the sink. "Would you sell a half-interest in this place for that kind of money?"

Scott was incredulous. "Are you kidding? That's seventy-five per cent of what the property would fetch under the hammer. Who would I sell to?"

Usher's gesture made nonsense of mathematics. "Me. A half-interest in everything, Jamie. House, yard, horses. I wasn't kidding last night. There'll be money to spare."

Scott's hope shrivelled. He made a sound of disgust.

Usher took it in good part. "I'm not a one-shot artist, make no mistake, I'll have the money. There'll be that much more in the kitty if you come in with me. I can't operate alone. All you're doing is sticking cash into somebody else's pocket. Think about it that way."

Scott opened the door to the stableyard. They were acting like two bums who find a sweepstake ticket—arguing whether the Rolls they will buy should be blue or black.

"Let's go. Maybe veal-and-ham pie will take your mind off high finance."

They jolted down the lane to the vicarage wall and into The Mall. The short wide street finished at the churchyard. The bench where in summer old men warmed their bones was empty. Two women stood among unkempt grass and headstones, shushing a child to decent silence. The stretch from church to inn was deserted. Beyond the ugliness of the gas station, Mrs. Parrish's mirror glinted like a watchful eye.

Usher pointed at it. " She ought to have two of them. One facing this way. She's missing half the action."

Scott pulled on to the tarmac in front of the pub. " Eternity, that's why. She claims she'll be long enough in her grave without wasting her time looking at it."

Usher ran his fingers through his hair, straightened his tie. He looked at the parked cars with interest.

" Bentleys, no less. What your father would have called ' Ostentatious farmings '."

Scott slammed the heavy door of the Land-Rover behind him. Every car on the lot had climbed the lane to Chestnut Gate at least once—but not any more. The stink of failure was apparently offensive.

" They don't farm. They clip dividend coupons."

The room was long under a low, fake-beam ceiling. The walls were festooned with horse-bronzes and hunting prints. A panelled bar faced the leaded windows overlooking the parking lot. The atmosphere smelled rich—as if the essence of cigar-smoke, scent and Scotch were piped through the hot air ducts. A small group of people stood in front of the open fireplace. The women wore a Mayfair interpretation of country attire. The men were in Sulka neck-scarves and cavalry-twill trousers. The hard bright voices faltered at Scott's arrival, regaining momentum like a sound-track stopped and restarted.

The woman behind the bar had dark red hair above a dead-white face. Her soft flesh rolled a little where nipped by her dress. A coloured stone of improbable dimensions flashed on her left hand. She took a hard look at Usher before greeting Scott.

" Hello, Jamie."

His smile was guarded. It was two months since he'd set foot in the place but one Sunday morning was like another. The same loud-mouths were there, talking without listening, advertising personal success. The horses they backed invariably won. If they bought stock, it jumped five points overnight. They brought their sleek bodies and shiny automobiles into the village for an hour every week—like kept women returning to queen it over the shopgirls.

He ordered his drink. " Could you do a couple of lunches as well, Lallie? I'm stuck."

She turned her back, moulded curves working as she fixed the Tom Collins. He watched her face in the mirror warily. Her eyes flicked sideways to the tallest man in the group in front of the fire. He had the soft white hair and pink stare of the albino. He teetered a little on long legs, taken with the anecdote he was relating. The woman pushed the drinks across the bar. She spoke through a fixed smile.

" Be careful, Jamie."

The two men sat in the barrel chairs by the window. Usher speared a cocktail onion, mouth wry as he bit into it.

" Be careful! What's that in aid of?"

Scott shrugged. It had been a mistake to come. Now it was too late to leave.

" The character's the major. Jack Mellor. Her husband. We're not exactly chummy. Sunday mornings, he's not usually here."

Usher swivelled slowly in his chair. As if the movement were his cue, Mellor left his audience. He emptied his glass at the bar and asked his wife for another. He made certain he was heard by the entire room.

" Mr. Scott is buying this one."

He came across to the table, broad-shouldered in a check jacket. A pale fuzz peeped from his open shirt neck. His teeth were too small for his heavy jaw.

" I thought you'd like me to have a drink, Jamie."

Adrenalin rushed in Scott's veins. But he controlled his voice.

" Any time. Any time you think you need one."

Mellor pondered the implication then turned to Usher.

" I'm Jack Mellor. I have to get in when I can with Jamie.
We don't see much of him these days."

Usher crossed his legs easily. His weight hung poised in
the tilted chair.

" You know something—I can't think of any good reason
why you should."

Only Scott recognised the hidden menace. The others
heard no more than the mildness of his cousin's voice.

"Why don't you go back to your friends, Jack?" Scott
asked quietly.

Mellor swayed out of perpendicular, his expression cunning. " But we're *all* friends here, aren't we, Lallie?" The
woman's hand reached out as though at ten feet she could
restrain him. Mellor switched his attention back to Usher.
" I didn't get your name."

The smile grew on Usher's face. " That's because I didn't
give it to you."

Mellor's skin flamed. He muttered something and hurried into the centre of lowered voices by the fire.

Usher let his chair to the floor, frowning into his glass.
" What's with him—the wife?"

The drink was clean on Scott's palate. " She used to
come out to see the horses work. He thinks I laid her."

Usher's eyes were innocent. " And did you?"

Scott shook his head. " She's not my type." He carried
the empty glasses over for a refill. The gesture seemed to
magnetise Mellor back to their table. He leant both hands
on the wood, talking like a man who needs to explain. His
diction was careful.

" We see little of Jamie because he's saving to pay his
debts. He's a rotten trainer. Do you know why he's a rotten
trainer—because he tries to mix business with pleasure. Ask
him whether he can pay his debts," he invited. He straightened up, wagging a finger with a drunk's solemnity.

Usher's voice was loud and distinct. " You're loaded and
you bother me. Shove!"

Mellor's eyes narrowed. " Now look here—I run a pub

39

for decent people, not riffraff." He slewed towards his cronies, inviting their approval. Suddenly he took both glasses from the table and emptied the contents on the floor. " Now get out!"

A woman's laugh exploded in the sudden silence. Usher moved with savage speed. He knelt under the thrashing arm, caught it and jerked Mellor's body forward. The man's legs flailed the air. The crash of his landing shook the bottles behind the bar. Usher hauled him to his feet, pinning him against the wall by the throat.

"Next time I'll break your arm," he promised.

The room was silent again till they left. They sat in the Land-Rover watching the pub door. They heard someone fasten it from the inside. The curtains moved furtively. Scott groped for the ignition keys.

" I'm sorry, Craig. We should never have gone there. Mellor's just capable of taking out a summons for assault."

Usher's face was unconcerned. "I doubt it. He threw the first punch." His voice changed. " I've seen you half-kill a guy for less. What happened to you, Jamie?"

Scott rammed into low gear. He turned the vehicle into the road, taking the bend out of the village at speed. His only thought was that each yard gained took him farther from this last humiliation. Usher stretched his legs as far as they would go. His head was tilted back, his eyes shut. He seemed to accept Scott's mood and choice of destination without more comment.

Past the sawmill, a stone boundary wall followed the winding road for a half-mile. Scott pulled on to the gravelled space in front of closed iron gates. The windows of the small lodge were uncurtained. A driveway on the far side of the gates disappeared into a beech thicket. Through bare branches, an expanse of parkland was visible, the elegant outline of a Georgian dwelling. No smoke came from the chimney-stacks. Both house and grounds had the still, forsaken quality of a property deserted.

Usher moved lazily, eyes suddenly alert. He opened the

door and climbed out. He stood in front of the gates, staring down the weed-grown driveway. He strolled back to the car and resumed his seat.

"That's where the dog took me this morning. Through your back paddock and over a trout stream. Whose is it?"

Scott answered with a sense of anti-climax. "The galloping major's. At least, his wife's. They lived there till he took over the pub. All things considered, it's as well nobody saw you."

Usher was frankly indifferent. "Is it for sale?"

In spite of himself, Scott treated the inquiry seriously. "All hundred and twenty acres of it. A house riddled with dry-rot and full of Victorian furniture. They're asking ten thousand. Six would buy it."

Usher's fingers were drumming on the dashboard. The frown lines deepened on his forehead as if he were committing the sum to memory. Scott let his breath go. It was time to say his piece. Any sort of gamble was better than waiting for an end that would strip him of everything, including his self-respect. When you were fighting for your life, help was where you found it.

"You might as well know it, Craig. I'm in trouble with the tax authorities as well as the bank. Last night I realised I've been kidding myself. I've only got one way out—your way. If you want me with you, I'll be glad of the chance. Yesterday taught me something. I need a guilty conscience like a hole in the head. I just got rid of mine back in that bar."

Usher accepted the news impassively. He rubbed a hand through his bristle of hair, thumb and forefinger finding the width of the white streak with practised ease.

"How much are you in for and how long have you got?"

For the second time that day, figures made no sense. What did make sense was a batch of cancelled cheque stubs. Entrance fees, oats, groceries. In spite of what Craig might think, he hadn't spent a week away from Chestnut Gate since he'd moved in.

"Sixteen hundred before the end of the month," he answered.

Usher was busy now, manicuring his nails with the end of the ignition key. He might have been commenting on the weather.

"They'll send you broke if you don't pay. You know that, of course."

Scott sat a little straighter. This was less the welcome fanfare than the roll of drums before the head falls.

"Sure I know it. Is that all you've got to say?"

Usher was still intent on his nails, head down. "What changed your mind—those clowns back there? I need to know."

There was a hint of judgment in his cousin's voice that Scott found worrying. He did his best to answer honestly.

"Last night scared me, Craig. I'm over it now. Maybe I needed that jolt. I never thought I'd be a bum in my own village."

"Everyone's scared," said Usher. "Except the lunatics who make things tough for the rest of us. That isn't what worried me—it's your moral compunctions. What I propose doing is a lot different to wheeling a safe out of an empty apartment. This is grabbing a guy in broad daylight. Tying him up, gagging him, till I've used his keys. That means as little or as much violence as is necessary. The risk is bigger—so is the pay-off. I can't afford a mistake, Jamie."

Scott watched the rook plane through the beeches, its cry raucous as it scattered the sparrows on the edge of the gravel. He tried for the right answer.

"Chestnut Gate means more than just five years' savings. It's every goddam dream I have. I've given my animals good food and an honest run—no fooling around with chemistry sets and tranquillisers. I had to go broke to get the message. You needn't worry about me, Craig. I'm converted."

Usher stuck the key back in the ignition lock. His tone allowed no doubt of his determination.

"Then that makes two of us. This is my Swan Song, as they say. There's more to it than just getting the money, Jamie. I meant what I said. I want an equal share in Chestnut Gate. You and I could swing it together."

The prospect excited Scott. Over the years, the bond between them had stretched but never snapped. Too many good memories belonged to them both. Burns Night at the Mapleleaf Stadium, his father standing between them, sternly proud of the kilt each wore. Years later, the dusty McLaughlin-Buick, parked where he and Craig lay in the grass with the Torrance girls. The Top-Hat Club—Craig flushed, defiant and generous, the night he'd broken his trust fund.

Scott's voice was louder than he intended. "You're damn' right it'll work. What the hell else is there left?"

Usher glanced at his watch. "It means a change in my schedule. I'd better get back to town as soon as I can. Don't worry about lunch. I'll grab something on the train."

Scott switched on the motor. "There's an express gets you into Waterloo just after three."

Usher frowned. "How well do you know a trainer called Fogarty?"

It was more than just a name. It stood for everything Scott had hoped to be and have. A string of good horses, owners who raced for the love of the sport. A record of Gold Cups won and a reputation for integrity.

"Only by sight. You're not going to grab him?"

Usher's hands were restless again. "No, not him. Would he recognise your horsebox?"

The suggestion was ridiculous. At any other time, Scott would have laughed. "Hell, no. How would he? I don't suppose he's ever seen it in his life."

Usher ducked his head in satisfaction. "Then we're really in business. With any sort of luck I should have news by to-night. I'll call you late."

Scott put the vehicle in gear. There were twenty-one days to the end of the month. He hid the anxiety in his voice.

"When do you think—I mean, how soon would we operate?"

Usher's eyes were bird-bright. "This week," he said confidently.

# CRAIG USHER

He jumped from the bus at the lights, ignoring the coloured conductor's protests. The boards outside the Albert Hall advertised a piano recital. The queue of Bach lovers reached half-way round the circular building. He hurried by, crossing the expanse of Queen's Gate. There he turned south into a row of mews houses, stopping at the last on his left. The lantern over the blue door was lighted. Set in the wall above the bellpush was a Spanish tile, its colours vivid, its message banal. *Pan, salud y amor.* He touched the button. A chime sounded upstairs. Easing a hand through the flap in the mailbox, he fished out a key on a string. He opened the door and threw his overcoat on the tallboy in the tiny hall. A girl's voice called and he answered. He climbed the short serpentine staircase.

The first he saw of Caroline Woodall were her mocassined feet and check-trousered legs. His eyes lifted to the dull-red silk shirt then to her face. She had grey eyes and a thin nose, finely-textured skin that would wrinkle at thirty. Her shoulder-length hair was skewered into a fudge-coloured bun.

He touched her cheek with his mouth. The room was warm and gay with floral chintz. A gate-legged table was set for two people. Through the half-open door was a glimpse of an ivory bedroom. A record-player offered the unexpected sequences of a Shearing solo. For a girl of twenty-four, she had a flair for atmosphere beyond her years, he thought. She relied on tested factors. Music, drink and food had all been approved by him at some time or other. Then inexperience betrayed her. She still lacked the tact to hide her emotions.

He tilted the bottle of Canadian Club, weakening its strength with water. She watched him, unsmiling. He recognised the symptoms. If he poured for her, she'd refuse. She would drink when good and ready and not before. He set his glass by a vase top-heavy with roses. A pan spattered in the kitchen. She didn't miss a trick. They'd eat curried prawns on plain rice, guavas, and drink Rhine wine. He nodded his appreciation, widening his nostrils.

" Smells good. Why don't I eat here more often?"

She poured herself a modest gin-and-tonic. She handled her slim, wiry body with a minimum of effort.

" I won't try to answer that."

He eyed her quizzically. " I detected the frost warning on the phone, a couple of hours ago. All right, let's get it over—which is it—what I have done or what I haven't done?"

She disappeared into the bedroom. The volume of music was lessened. She came back, her piled hair heavy on her slender neck.

" You know I'm not very good at this sort of thing, Craig. You couldn't come home with me because you were supposed to be in the country until to-morrow. So Mother came up for the week-end. She spent the whole time lecturing me about the dangers of associations with older men. You chose the wrong moment to phone. She was here. She's worried about me."

He helped himself to more ice. " I'm sorry about that. How about you, are you worried?"

She made a sound of exasperation. " Don't be difficult. Part of the trouble is that she likes you. You flatter her, say all the right things. That's precisely what both her husbands did. Can't you see that's why she's worried?"

He shrugged. " She's your mother—I've been a guest in her house. She also happens to be fifteen years older than I am. I treat her accordingly. What's her complaint?"

She fingered the topaz on her right hand nervously. " You're being deliberately obtuse. It's me. You've heard her on the subject—you've even agreed with her. She's against everything I've done for the last three years. Secretarial college, living alone in London, taking a job."

"But the real road to ruin is a forty-year-old Canadian who is civil to her—is that it?" He patted the padded bench-seat.

She came to join him. Her face was anxious and devoid of coquetry.

"*Please* try to understand, Craig. I'm her only child. All she wants is to see me happy."

The implication nettled him in spite of its justice. A chance meeting at a cocktail party had started it all. For nine months he'd given what he had to offer with no thought other than the hope that it would last. They'd shared a happy summer. Long, lazy evenings, the curtains blowing in the other room, their bodies responsive on the bed. She had accepted what little he told her of himself unquestioningly, content that he ate the food she prepared. Week-ends, they had escaped to the cool Kentish house, riding her mother's horses through the soft dust of hopfields. Six months ago, she'd found the job with Balaban Fine Gems. The change in their relationship had been subtle, as he became aware of the chance that she offered him. He told himself that he had never promised her more than he'd been prepared to give. That the blame belonged to the Fate Sisters. Love, with its connotation of sacrifice, was a word that bothered him. He cared enough for Caroline Woodall to hope that she would never know the truth about him.

"She wants to see you happy," he repeated. "What is it she's afraid of—that I'll ask you to marry me or that I won't?"

She looked at him steadily. "Aren't you being unfair?"

He lifted his shoulders. "Am I?"

She took his wrists in her hands, strong fingers forcing him to meet her intensity.

"Two men have lived on her money. My stepfather left

47

her with the house, barely enough to keep it going. She's terrified that the same thing will happen to me."

The muscles stiffened in his forearms. "For an old fortune-hunter, I must be losing my touch. Since when are you an heiress?"

She shook him gently. "Don't make it even worse than it is, Craig. My aunt left me ten thousand pounds. Mother doesn't know just how much of it has gone already. This house, the furniture. Just living. I don't care about it. But surely you can see how someone like my mother reasons?"

A simple yes or no solved nothing. Nothing short of the whole truth could justify him. All that summer, this small house had been a refuge from reality. A place in which to forget the dreariness of his room, the vigils in bushes, the endless fear of a hand tapping his shoulder. More than that, it had been a place where he felt wanted. Neither of them had ever mentioned money. Vaguely, he must have known that she could never have lived that way on her salary as secretary. He had shut his mind against the alternative. The balance of their relationhsip was set too fine to tip it without soul-searching.

"Let me ask you one thing—is it you or your mother who's really doing the worrying?"

She took away her hands. She refilled his glass, leaving her own empty.

"To-day and yesterday were absolute hell. I hated everything she said. Most of all the things she didn't say. But she's still my mother and I had to tell you. If you never want to see her again, I'll understand. Does that answer the question?"

She was standing over him, anxious and desirable. He put his cheek against her warm midriff.

"Things are going to be different," he promised without knowing what he really meant.

Her hands on the back of his neck were fiercely possessive. When at last he looked up, her face was tranquil. She smiled.

"I'll dish the food up. The wine's in the bath."

He emptied the ice bucket into the tub and wrapped a napkin round the slender bottle. The kitchen door was half-closed. He lit the spiral candles and moved without sound into the bedroom. The square divan was littered with clothes she had chosen and rejected. An oil painting of a fat grey pony hung at the side of the blue velvet curtains. By the bed, a heater matching the ivory furniture was humming busily. He stood in front of the dressing-table mirror. The angle of the kitchen door blocked him from her view. Her handbag was under a pile of stockings. He eased the catch open. The keys he sought were in a small zipped compartment. He slipped the matchbox from his pocket. One end of the box was broken away. The bottom half held a piece of cuttlefish bone. He sat on the stool, a comb stuck ready in his short hair in case the kitchen door moved. He pressed both keys into the matchbox, holding the wards flat on the cuttlefish bone. First a left profile and then a right. Finally he took a print of the diameter of each shank. The impressions were sharp and impervious to heat. He padded the matchbox with cotton and replaced it in his pocket. By the time she called him to take the plates, the keys were back in her bag. He carried the dishes from the kitchen. She switched off the wall-brackets, her face young in the candlelight.

"Did you have any luck with your agent?"

The fiction of writer had seemed easy to maintain. Few people knew what it implied. You put words on paper, sometimes they sold. She'd been content to let it go at that. He poured the pale-gold wine into the tall glasses.

"Ah—you know how it is. They never tell you anything definite. Something else came up. There's just a chance of a job with a guy I used to know."

She spread the curried prawns with shredded coconut and sliced banana. Her voice was studiously casual.

"In London?"

He bent over his food. "Why don't we talk about you? The subject's more interesting. How many tiaras did you sell this week?"

She held her fork in the air, frowning. "Do you know, it amazes me. I can't understand why Balaban bothers to go on. Everyone's against it. His doctors, his wife. He's supposed to take things easy. He's already had one coronary."

He wiped his mouth with his napkin. "To earn a living, maybe."

She turned down the corners of her mouth at the suggestion. "They don't have children. He's got more money than either of them can ever spend. In fact, I've reached the conclusion that he stays on in business for the sheer pleasure of refusing to sell."

"That's a twist," he said shortly.

She answered impatiently. "You don't understand. It's like working in an art gallery where nobody wants to part with the paintings. That's exactly what Balaban is—an artist. People come from Paris, New York—from Buenos Aires—to see his designs. Half the time, I know before I make the appointments that he has no intention of selling anything."

He killed the fire of the curry with a piece of bread. The chilled wine left his mouth tasting the grape.

"I don't know what your mother worries about. Your job sounds a cinch."

"It isn't just *this* job," she corrected. "It's any job. I ought to be at home with her, that's what she thinks. As it is, Balaban pays me twice what I'm worth. He no more needs a secretary than you do."

He'd assembled the picture over the months like a jigsaw puzzle. A chance word, a pointed question, added a key piece. Now it was almost complete. Balaban's safe held four items worth sixty thousand pounds. A pair of diamond ear-rings, a necklace, bracelet and ring in matched, flawless stones. For a year, Balaban had retained the set, stubbornly refusing to deliver it to the Amsterdam jeweller who had commissioned him. And there'd be more than just this in the safe.

" Who knows—maybe he hired you to talk horses," he said lightly. " He's an owner, isn't he?"

She smiled, the outside edges of her eyes lifting in a network of fine lines.

" I think I like Balaban better than any other man—excepting you. He's a fat, sentimental old fraud, most of the time. And he's completely unspoiled by success. He's kind, Craig. Enthusiastic about things and people. Now he's like a child with his horses."

He pushed his chair back and carried the plates into the kitchen. She turned up the record-player and started the coffee in the percolator. He folded the table and sat down beside her.

" Who was it you said trained for him?" he asked casually.

" Matt Fogarty. For an Irishman, he's long-suffering. Balaban's driving him out of his mind—getting up in the middle of the night and driving down to Epsom to watch the first ride-out. Can you imagine that for a trainer? Then he comes back to the office and repeats everything Fogarty's told him, upside down. The latest is that ' mares aren't as reliable as goldings.' He means geldings, of course."

He held her hand steady as she touched a match to his cigarette. The next question and answer were vital.

" I can imagine he'd be popular with Fogarty. You're not going to tell me that he goes down there every day?"

She slid her body on to the bench-seat, stretched out and crossed her ankles in his lap.

" He knows he's outworn his welcome but he still goes. He's so obstinate, Craig. The new horse runs in a hurdle at Sandown on Thursday. Balaban has the idea that it works better if he's watching. He doesn't know the first thing about racing and he's sweet."

51

He stretched out his arm, depositing his coffee-cup on the table. There were three days left. Monday, Tuesday and Wednesday—that was assuming Fogarty didn't work the animal on the day it ran. He lifted her feet to the ground and kissed her.

"It's gone ten. I'm going to have to run."

She smoothed the hair straying on her neck, her voice hesitant. "I thought you might stay. Ah well. When do I see you again?"

He put his hands in his jacket pocket, fingering the match-box. Caroline was Balaban's employee. The cops would interrogate her, that much was certain. Not that she ran any danger. There were people in and out of the office all day long. Any one of a dozen tipsters in the business could have visited the premises and put-up the job. Still more important—there was no cause for the police to suspect him. They reasoned according to rule. The tradition was that thieves varied neither crime nor method. Pickpockets didn't peddle phoney stock and con-men stayed away from blowing safes. The police would be looking for the heavy mob—the strong-arm specialists, not a guy with a burglary record. His face wouldn't be seen—nobody would hear his voice. The alibi he had worked out would be his final assurance.

"Why don't I just call you?" he said easily. "You know the way it is—I'm hoping for news of that job I told you about. It may come to-morrow—the next day. I don't want to tie myself up in case I have to go for an interview."

She stood on tiptoe, whispering and nibbling at his ear. She let him go, her eyes searching.

"You're not cross at anything I said? It's still the same, isn't it, Craig?"

"The same as ever, sweetie," he lied. Somehow, he had to salvage the best of what was left between them. "I'll call you," he repeated.

She followed him down the stairs. She held his over-coat, touching the pinned tear in the sleeve.

"You're careless with your clothes, Craig. That safety-pin looks terrible."

"A nail," he said casually. "I'll drop it off at the cleaners to-morrow."

At the end of the mews, he turned round. She was still standing in the open doorway. He raised a hand and hurried north towards Kensington High Street.

A telephone in the subway station was vacant. He dialled Scott's number, presenting a blank face to the girls giggling in the neighbouring booth. There was a village operator to eavesdrop. His message was laconic.

"Meet me at four o'clock to-morrow. In the Reading Room. You won't be getting back till late so make whatever arrangements are necessary."

Scott's answer was even shorter. "Check. Four o'clock."

Usher hung up, his eyes thoughtful. This sounded like the old Jamie, relaxed and dependable. He dropped a coin into the ticket machine and boarded a District Line train. At Earl's Court station, he pushed his way through the crowd blocking the exit. The street-scene was lively—Poles, Greeks and negroes lolled against the closed store windows. Indian women fluttered by, their western shoes strangely drab under the vivid splendour of their saris. A ring of Salvationists stood on the street kerb outside, witnessing the Blood of the Lamb to the accompaniment of a slide-horn. The pubs had emptied into the coffee-bars. Earl's Court Road was vulgar and vital—still staving off the misery of Monday morning.

Usher cut east, turning into the gloomy Victorian square. The steps of the house where he lived were stuck with paper and leaves. Dirty milk bottles made the way up perilous. He let himself into the dim hallway. The stairs ran out of carpet on the second floor. He opened the door at the back of the landing and switched on the light. The house rules were simple. Rent was paid weekly in advance —tenants received neither coloured nor Asiatic visitors in their rooms—no washing was hung from the windows.

The management lived in the basement flat—a woman with a goitre and dirty ankles who kept too many cats. Each tenant did his own chores.

He looked round the small room. There was no reason for anyone to have been there. The quick, assessing stare when he came home had become second nature to him. Everything was as he had left it. The three packed suitcases were stacked on top of one another—ready for collection by a man whose pockets should have been stuffed with the contents of the Cockburn safe. He lowered the blind and sat on the bed. The disaster of the previous night had shaken him more than he had shown. They had both come desperately close to the banging of a cell door. What mattered more was the lack of foresight that had put them in jeopardy. It was going to be different with Balaban. He'd check every factor, human and mechanical. And when that was done, he'd check again.

He opened the door quietly. The sounds were familiar. Across the landing, the grunt-and-swing of the law student working out on his rowing-machine. The yowl of a cat locked either out or in came from downstairs. The typing on the top floor was frantic in an attempt to beat the house deadline for noise. He tiptoed up the short flight. Mrs. Sangster's door would be fastened and wedged to repel an unlikely assault. Three more steps took him to the communal bathroom. He shut himself in. The water-soaked floor, the female hair festooning the hand-basin, made light of the printed admonition to cleanliness. He unfastened the inspection hatch in the panelling that enclosed the dirt-ringed tub. The explosive-looking geyser over his head leaked incessantly.

He pushed his hand past twisted plumbing till his fingers found the heavy sponge-bag. Back in his room, he emptied the contents on the bed. A small vice, several types of files and a couple of dozen skeleton keys. He screwed the vice to the mantel, padding the clamps with paper to avoid scarring the paintwork. Choosing two of the skeleton keys,

he fitted their heads delicately into the moulds he had
made. The sharp impressions bore the usual embellish-
ments designed to give the original key importance. But
all keys conformed to the same principle, to one of several
basic patterns. This type was a raised E. He measured the
wards with a pair of callipers. One of his keys matched its
mould perfectly. The other was too thick on its inside edge.
He fastened the shank in the vice. Holding the file flat, he
cut the key with short sure strokes till the measurements
satisfied him. The final job was accurate. He rubbed the
metal surfaces smooth with emery-paper and put the two
keys in the dressing-table drawer. The tools he had used,
the ring of spare keys, he replaced in the sponge-bag. The
staircase was quiet and empty. He returned the bag to its
hiding place and made ready for bed.

# CRAIG USHER

He woke, as usual, to the slap of the woman's slippers across the landing. He lay where he was till he heard her climbing the stairs—then opened his door. Mrs. Sangster was forty-ish. She carried two milk bottles, clutched against her wrapper. Her hair was in a net and her eyes bagged with fatigue. She was breathless.

"These stairs will kill me yet, I know it. Now listen—you didn't say you were going to be away last night. I left your milk as usual. It was still there when I came back from church. Somebody must have taken it later—pigs!"

It was six months since he had discovered the milk bottle left outside his door for the first time. Since then a routine had been established. They met briefly for a few minutes every morning. Had he seen her dressed for the street, he doubted whether he would have recognised her. He took his half-pint pointing at the closed door across the landing.

"My money's on the athlete—he probably trains on the stuff. How'd your pools go?"

Once a week, she invested God knows what percentage of her salary in football-pools—unhinged for life by a chance win of seventy pounds. She pulled the wrapper closer, speaking with implicit faith in fortune merely delayed.

"Nineteen points again. And who do you think let me down?"

He gave her the seriousness she demanded. "Birmingham?"

Her mouth was acid. "Naturally. Ah well. *Pisces* is in the ascendant. I know you laugh at 'Stars make your Decisions,' but you'll see."

He closed the door on her firmly. All over the city, people were bracing themselves against the deadliness of their existence with a dream. They clutched at the skirts of the Fate Sisters, pleading for the right results in a permutation of football games—a horse of their choice to get its number into the winner's frame—a roulette wheel to stop turning where they willed. Meanwhile, the bookmakers and pool and wheel-operators wintered in Jamaica. None of the suckers had discovered the only gamble valid. Your liberty against a worthwhile haul.

He filled the tin kettle and set it on the gas-ring. The same water served to boil an egg, make tea and lather his face for shaving. The grey hopsack suit was freshly pressed. In spite of what Caroline said, his wardrobe had been carefully conserved. Clothes were as much tools of his trade as the keys in the dressing-table drawer. He chose a blue shirt and a knitted silk tie. He unlocked one of the suitcases. Under the jumble of socks and ties was a small leather folder. He unzipped it. The thin sheaf of fivers was on top of his passport. He counted his reserve. It was woefully small. He peeled off six bills and relocked the suitcase. The keys made a pleasant jingle in his hand—functional yet elegant. He shook up his bed, put the milk bottle on the window-sill and went downstairs.

A sombre sky poised menacing clouds. The seven o'clock news had threatened the possibility of snow. Beyond the square, the Earl's Court Road was already dealing with another week. Nobody loitered in the raw morning. There were queues at the bus-stops. The subway sucked in the second of the eastbound rushes, timing it to arrive in the City around nine-thirty. A few street pedlars were assembling their stands, their handcarts loaded with fruit and flowers. In front of the cut-price store, a man was taking down the window shutters. Usher turned the corner, past the smell of wet fish and stale reek of the silent pub. A few more days and he'd be out of it, leaving these strained, unsmiling faces to the rat-race. Thought of the countryside warmed him. He hailed a cab with a sense of sudden affluence.

The park was sad with winter, the brown turf deserted. Water-fowl cruised over the edges of the Serpentine. A troop of Household Cavalry trotted along the South Carriageway, their accoutrements brilliant in the grey day. An audience of nursemaids and children hurried after them. A block north of Oxford Street, Usher tapped on the glass and paid off his driver. He walked rapidly up Marylebone Lane. A hundred yards on, he turned west and into a small office building. The familiar sign was still screwed to the first door along the corridor.

COMMON MARKET RESEARCH COMPANY LTD.

He entered the office, removing his hat as the girl looked up from her typewriter. She was new and unfamiliar. He smiled.

" Mr. Van der Pouk?"

She let her cigarette fall into her tea-cup with a bored gesture. Her black hair was wound into a tall pompadour, her mask of make-up registering regret. " I'm afraid Mr. Van der Pouk is busy at the moment. Do you have an appointment?"

It took an effort to stay civil. " I imagine you'd know if I had. Just tell him Mr. Curtis is here—the Toronto Fidelity Corporation."

She swayed to an inner door, preserving her portrayal of a sophisticate caught in vulgar circumstances. She was gone no more than half a minute. Her invitation was delivered with a little more enthusiasm.

" Will you come this way, Mr. Curtis?"

Usher's feet bedded in soft carpet. A fumed oak cupboard stood in the corner of the room, a Regency table served as a desk. A man sat behind it, his back to the purple-and-gold of the pot plants on the window ledge. He wore a fine, brown suit and sober linen. Nose and brow were those of a head on a Roman coin. Seeing Usher, he half-rose from his chair, his short arms lifted as though weighing an invisible burden. His accented voice was polite.

"This is a pleasure, Mr. Curtis." The girl hesitated in the doorway. He scribbled something on an envelope. "Take this to the post office, Miss Abel. You must register it and bring me the receipt."

Usher took the vacant seat. Neither man spoke till they heard the girl's heels click along the corridor. Van der Pouk spoke with soft regret, worrying his left ear.

"This is foolish, Craig. I do not want you here."

Usher opened the cigarette box on the table. "You wouldn't have wanted me at your home either. What I've got to say isn't for the phone."

Van der Pouk looked at the instrument with mistrust. He shifted his glance to the wall decorations. The statistical charts and stock-market graphs were done on thick cartridge paper. He seemed to gather conviction from the sight.

"We have not seen one another for over a year. I do no more of that business, Craig. Times change."

Usher smiled. "They do indeed. Me too, I'm retiring."

The Belgian's heavy shoulders lifted. He took the news sceptically. "This is what you came to tell me?"

Usher stretched out his legs, considering the tips of his shoes. "No, Jean, not exactly. All the years I've known you, you've never been cheap. Sharp, yes. You made a fair profit out of me. But you didn't cheat and you kept your mouth shut. That's why I'm here. I thought you'd like to know I'm not retiring empty-handed."

"Ah, *bon*," said Van der Pouk. He rested the top half of his body on his forearms, thrusting out his massive head. "You know the saying, of course. A man goes only so often to the well. I was very lucky, Craig. Now it pleases me to forget those times. Do you understand?"

The smile on Usher's face was fixed. "*Merde!* You

couldn't pay that outraged duchess outside on what this office earns. What you really mean is that you don't go to the well so often. You've become more selective. I like that, Jean. But it's a good job I'm not the law. I've a nose for these things. And I read my newspapers. I want to bet you've handled most of the coups that have been going off."

Van der Pouk juggled the suggestion before dealing with it. "You have not lost your taste for fantasy, Craig. Even if this were true, it would change nothing. Your business ceased to be interesting a long time ago. I hope I make myself clear. I have no wish to give offence."

Usher accepted the criticism without showing rancour. Strictly on the record, the Belgian was right. A run of bad luck had forced him into stupid ventures—haphazard assaults on houses with no real idea of what he was doing. Inevitably, the booty had been rubbish. Van der Pouk had bought what was offered a couple of times. The assumption was that he preferred this to straightforward charity. Finally the Belgian had refused to compromise himself further. Usher was flat-broke when he read of the Millet Fowlers' absence advertised in the social column of *The Times*. He'd dropped thirty feet through a skylight into the Park Lane apartment to find a collection of empty jewel cases. In the back of a writing-bureau he'd discovered enough Swiss francs to ensure a meagre living for a limited time. He'd awakened the next morning dehydrated, depressed and disgusted with himself. The same afternoon, he moved everything he owned into the room in Earl's Court. Ever since then, his future had been planned with Spartan discipline.

"I've learned, Jean. I've come to you because this is big. I don't know anyone else who could produce the sort of money I need."

Footsteps were loud in the corridor. Van der Pouk was prudent until they stopped in a neighbouring office. He leaned across his desk, supporting his chins in cupped hands.

His eyes were shrewd. "What is the nature of this merchandise?"

"Gem quality diamonds," Usher said quickly. "Cut stones in their settings. Sixty thousand pounds worth, certainly. Maybe more."

The Belgian rose to his feet. Erect, he appeared even more solid. He turned a flower-pot on the window-sill so that the foliage shared the light. The back of his head was almost neckless, tough brown hair growing down as far as his collar.

"I take it that these articles are not in your possession."

The skeleton keys were smooth under Usher's fingers. "Let's say I've got control of them. Complete control. You could be on the plane for Brussels before they were missed."

Van der Pouk turned the last flower-pot. He had the clipped confidence of a lecturer sure of his facts.

"Stones like this are readily identified, Craig. They are weighed, the cut and fashion of the facets recorded. In some cases even the internal structure of the stone is X-rayed."

Usher smiled. "I've heard you on the subject before. That's why you'll offer me half of what they're worth. I'm quoting you the valuation for insurance. None of this stuff is overrated, Jean. I'm going to put a price on it—there'll be no haggling. There's enough in it for everybody. Thirty thousand pounds."

Van der Pouk wiped his fingers on his handkerchief. He phrased his next sentence delicately.

"Suppose I *were* interested—how soon would you need this money? Such a sum would take time to produce."

Usher stood up in turn. "To-morrow," he said flatly. "To-morrow morning. I don't care what currency I'm paid in as long as it's in used bills. If you can't meet that deadline, I'd better know now."

Van der Pouk opened a cupboard. He poured himself a glass of white wine, held it to the light.

61

"We have had differences of opinion," he said judiciously. "But we have always been truthful with one another. This is a great deal of money. I will have to satisfy my associates that the merchandise exists. How can you help me there? They are—you know the word—*sérieux*."

"We all are," Usher said shortly. "I can deliver tomorrow morning without any fuss. That's as much as I'm prepared to say. If it isn't enough for your friends, we'll forget it. I'll try to get action somewhere else."

The Belgian made a wry mouth—as if the wine were sour to his palate. He hurried his answer as the door banged in the outer office.

"I will buy what you have to sell."

"Fair enough. You can make your plane reservation for to-morrow morning, if you like," said Usher. "Any time after nine-thirty. We'll fix the details later. I'll be in the Hyde Park Buttery at half past six to-night. The man who'll be with me is my partner."

Van der Pouk's jowls quivered. "I never talk business in front of strangers, Craig."

Usher removed the Belgian's hand from his sleeve. "This isn't a stranger. I've known him all my life. He's the one who'll deliver. He's got to know what you look like."

Van der Pouk's head shot into the shelter of his shoulders like that of a tortoise. "Aha. Then be discreet. Do not come here any more and do not telephone. I will see you at half past six."

# CRAIG USHER

The window table where they sat was level with the top decks of the passing buses. It was on the stroke of five and the dingy restaurant was deserted. Behind them, the only waitress on duty was clattering crockery through a service-hatch—the noise a reminder that it was almost closing-time. Both men had a clear view of the junction of Hatton Garden and High Holborn.

Usher lit a fresh cigarette from the stub of the last, his eyes on the car circling the block. It slowed in front of the grey-stone office building. Scott used a newspaper to clear a space on the steamed window.

" That's the third time that car's passed since we've been sitting here."

The vehicle was parked in defiance of traffic regulations. Squat and sinister.

Usher nodded. " It's the Flying Squad. But don't let it bother you. They don't know we exist."

Scott's thin brown face was enigmatic. " They're there, aren't they? What are they looking for—jay-walkers?"

Usher shrugged. The explanation was too involved. The law wasn't interested in the respectable façade of Hatton Garden. The names of the wholesale diamond merchants and assay offices were synonymous with integrity. It was the sidewalks that were suspect—the smoke-filled cafés where untaxed goods changed hands—the doorway dealers offering smuggled watches and stolen jewellery.

"Don't let it bother you," he repeated. The end of Scott's thick eyebrows grew up towards his temples, giving him a saturnine expression.

" Do I look particularly worried?" he asked.

Usher treated the question literally. The years had dug deep lines from the other's nose to his mouth—leaving scowl marks between the eyes. The straight, fair hair had thinned a little. The grey suit Scott was wearing had been cut by a good tailor. The trench-coat and decently-battered hat were inconspicuous.

He delivered judgment. "I'll tell you what you look like. A perfectly respectable citizen who wouldn't know a squad car if it ploughed up his front lawn. Keep that in your head and you've got no problems."

The waitress folded the last tablecloth. Apart from the two men sitting at the window, the room was empty. Usher asked for the check, adding a couple of shillings to the modest sum.

"We're on our way," he assured her.

She smiled mechanically and left them in peace. Across the street, the police car was still stationary in front of the office building.

"Another couple of minutes," Usher said confidently.

A match snapped in Scott's restless fingers. "What if she's late?"

"Caroline's never late," answered Usher. "Everyone's out of that building at six. The caretaker locks the street door dead on the hour. That's the only key we don't have. We're going in whether the law's still sitting there or not." He was on his feet even as he spoke. They hurried down the stairs to the street. A few yards away, an arcade offered shelter. They stood out of sight watching the east-west traffic stop for the lights. A phalanx of workers rushed the crossing, making for bus, subway and taxi. The long-legged girl in the suède coat turned right and took her place in the queue. She battled her way forward, neither giving nor asking quarter till she hauled herself on to the platform of a South Kensington bus. The two men stayed concealed till the vehicle was out of sight. Usher hurried to the corner pay-phone. Scott joined him in the stuffy booth.

Usher dialled a number, holding the instrument so Scott could hear the ringing at the other end. The summons went unanswered. He replaced the phone.

" We walk in together. No gloves till we're in the building. Whatever happens, don't turn your head as you pass them—as far as you're concerned, it's just another parked car."

Scott touched the brim of his hat self-consciously. Any strain he might be feeling was well camouflaged. They side-stepped through the traffic to the far side of the street. The squad car was only twenty feet away. Rear doors and window were fitted with bloomed glass. Vision was only possible from the inside out. They walked down Hatton Garden, close enough to the prowl car to hear the radio operator's monotonous call. Usher put a foot on the bottom step up to the office entrance. Without looking, he knew what was happening behind him. The two cops sitting in front would be watching every passer-by—assessing their appearance. Trained to detect the least sign of guilt. In spite of his warning to Scott, the urge to turn his own head and face danger was strong. The nine steps seemed endless. The lobby was still busy with homebound workers. The two men mingled with the crowd, skirted the elevator, unhurried and unremarked. The staircase was deserted. They climbed as far as the third floor and turned into a corridor where the lights still burned. Usher led the way to a pair of doors facing one another. He opened the nearer on a room barely larger than a cupboard. There was a sink with faucets, a pile of stacked buckets and mops. An electric sweeper and polisher stood in the corner. He pulled on his gloves.

" Keep out of sight while I attend to the door. As soon as I open it, all hell will break loose—the burglar alarm. At this time of day, nobody'll pay any attention. When you see me in, you follow. O.K.?"

Scott's eyes flickered as the elevator rattled up. Across

the corridor a typewriter still clattered. A woman's body was silhouetted against the ground glass twelve feet away. He nodded, his tongue nervous on his lips.

Usher stepped out. The door in front of him was solid and protected by two locks. He inserted the first key he had made. The levers lifted easily. He tried the second. This time, the wards fouled the mechanism of the lock. Sweat started under his arms, dripping icily against his rib-cage. He eased the key out gently and tried again, using lift with the turn. It revolved in a full circle. He pushed the door open. A bell vibrated on the outside wall of the building. He bent quickly, searching for the switch. He found it close to the floorboards, set in the wainscoting. He thumbed up the button. The clamour ceased. He stayed motionless, listening to the pattern of sound in the corridor. The noise of the alarm still persisted in his ears. Gradually the stuttering typewriter replaced it. He shut the door quickly as Scott joined him.

"Keep your voice down," he whispered. "There are people in the next office—and don't disturb anything."

There was enough light to discern the pleasant wallpaper, the comfortable furniture. The absence of office paraphernalia created an impression of a room lived in. The place smelled faintly of Caroline's scent. A single catalogue, printed in colour, lay on a glass-topped table. The legend across the front was in pica type.

joseph balaban fine jewels

He opened the door to the other office. The walls reflected the décor in contrasting shades. A modern desk was placed in front of the window so that natural light shed on its surface. Its only furnishings were a telephone, a leatherbound blotter and a pair of jeweller's scales. A silk curtain with Assyrian motif covered a niche on the inside wall. Usher pulled the cord. No more than the front of the massive safe was exposed. The rest was concreted into the structure of the building. The tiny keyhole was lost in an expanse of dull steel. Immediately above it, the handle was lodged at twelve o'clock. Usher touched the smooth metal with gloved fingers.

"You see why he locks up here and walks away happy? There are only two sets of keys. One's always on him—the other's kept at the bank. This box is impregnable. Gelignite—blowtorch—it's proof against everything. Two years old and cost the best part of a thousand pounds to install. You'll have it open in ten seconds."

Scott's head turned sharply. He swallowed very carefully before replying, "How do you mean, *I'll* have it open?"

Usher shifted his grip to the handle of the safe, ignoring the protest. He used his free hand to pantomime the insertion of a key into the tiny lock.

"I've read every bit of literature the makers put out on this baby. The key's double-ended like an old-fashioned watch key. You make one complete turn to the right then half a turn back—like that. It *stays* in the lock. You pull the handle down as far as it goes and the safe's open. Try it. Imagine you've got a key in your hand."

Scott's hesitation was only brief. Face hard in the half-light, he positioned himself in front of the safe. Again and again he repeated the drill till Usher was satisfied.

Usher made each word tell. "You take everything inside except the papers. When you've got what you want, lock the safe. It's the same thing in reverse. Handle up—key to the right then full circle left. Got it? Remember—one wrong move and you're in trouble. This box opens and shuts one way and one way only."

Scott pushed his hat back, rubbing the red line across his forehead. "What are you doing while I'm here opening the safe?"

Usher drew the silk curtain. "Making sure Balaban's under control."

"Why you not me?—you're supposed to be the pro."

Usher came a little nearer. "Let's say I'd rather have the responsibility." He jerked open the top drawer of the desk. Inside was a jumble of pencils and broken chesspieces—a cardboard clip of ampoules. A druggist's label was pasted across the container. He read the folder round the clip.

Amyl nitrate. For the relief of cardiac conditions.

Break the contents of the phial into a handkerchief and inhale.

He put the container back and shut the drawer. They went back to the other room. The rest of the floor was silent now though the elevator still rumbled at the end of the corridor. Scott perched his backside on the table, watching Usher without speaking. There was something stubbornly defiant about his posture—as if he would be happy to spend the night there. Put a hole in Jamie's conceit, thought Usher, and this is what you got. He acted quickly before it was too late.

"You know what this means to both of us, Jamie," he said quietly. "Only one can make the decisions. It has to be me."

The conciliation was enough to make Scott grin lop-sidedly.

"What else do I have to remember about this joint?"

Usher's wave took in the room. "The walls and furniture. Get them fixed in your head—so you could walk to that safe blindfolded if you had to. I'm going to take a chance and leave the alarm switched off. If anything should go wrong to-morrow morning, one of us'll have to get back here and switch it on again. Otherwise you turn it on when you leave. The caretaker doesn't live on the premises. He gets here at seven, unlocks the street door for the cleaners and takes off for breakfast. The women start their chores downstairs. You'll be out before they've reached the second floor."

Scott ran his hand down the inside of the door to the corridor. "What about this—how do I get it open?"

Usher turned the handle gently. The lights outside were cut. They stood in the silent darkness. Suddenly a cistern flushed in the lavatory a few feet away. Involuntarily, they moved closer to one another. The sound was repeated.

Usher relaxed. "Automatic."

He positioned Scott in front of the door, guiding his hands. "Hold the key like that, left forefinger under the shank. Now over easily—keep your wrist stiff. You've got to be able to *feel* the tumblers lift. Try again. Remember —time's going to count. There's none to spare."

Scott's movements grew surer. At the fifth attempt, he was locking and unlocking the door as quickly as his instructor. Usher dropped the two keys into his pocket, smiling.

"You want to make a little money on the side, you're ready to go into business on your own. Now listen. There's a good chance that one of the cleaners gets a look at you tomorrow. It means nothing as long as you don't open your mouth. Your general description's useless to the law. But if anyone gets a shot at your accent, the field's narrowed."

Scott's head nodded, understanding.

They walked the length of the dim passage, waited at the bottom of the stairs till they heard the elevator gates open. They joined the last stragglers crossing the lobby. Outside, the street lamps were on. Usher sheltered in the angle of the front doors, lighting a cigarette. His eyes searched both directions. The police car had gone. A couple of stooped janitors were hauling ash-cans across the pavement, ready for early-morning collection. Cats skirmished in the doorways. For the rest of the night, the devotion and ingenuity of police and security-guards would protect Europe's wealthiest diamond-brokers. Foot and mobile patrols, electronic devices, would guard the unpretentious-looking buildings. And to-morrow morning, Jamie would walk in and empty the safe as easily as Balaban himself.

The Buttery bar was almost empty. A couple of business men sat at the counter, grabbing half an hour's freedom between office and home. Usher and Scott chose a table at the far end of the room. The discreet lighting and service, the sound of modulated voices, were a relief after the strain of the last two hours. Usher lifted his glass. The first drink of the day was clean and fresh on his palate.

Scott looked at ease. He quoted, his eyes and mouth amused.

"'If Craig ever gets to Heaven, you'll find him reading the labels on the liquor bottles, one hand up an angel's skirt.' Remember the way Father always insisted that angels weren't sexless?"

The ice in Usher's glass rang like a bell. He could have done without evocation of the memory. Even after twenty years, dismissal by the family still rankled. Perhaps most of all, the macabre picture of Hogmanay in his uncle's house. For eighteen successive years, his place had still been set at table on New Year's Eve. The forbidden and invisible guest whose name must never be mentioned.

He spoke moodily. "Jehovah in a kilt—the hell with him. I've nothing to thank *him* for. Do you realise that we're the only human beings he couldn't make conform. It sent him crazy. He only kept himself alive till he knew I was in jail—then he died happy. You remember him the way you want. He was your father, not mine."

The lines were deep between Scott's eyes. "There's nothing happy about a man who blames himself for other people's mistakes. Not only mine but yours. He took two days dying, Craig—talking as if you were there with me, like an old, cracked record."

Usher looked at his watch. It was twenty past six. Ten minutes before Van der Pouk was due.

"What mistakes are you supposed to have made?" he asked sourly. "Go broke? He knew you'd never go into the business. Or did he think training racehorses was dishonest?"

"Let's drop it," Scott said quietly.

Usher put his glass on the table. "Sure I'll drop it—just leave me out of Happy Memory Hour. All I ever learnt from your father was the virtue of cold showers in an

Ontario winter. That and an ashplant across my arse at the age of seven. At times you sound as smug as he did. He thought everyone was capable of learning from experience except me. For all I know, that's your opinion too."

Scott's eyes were patient. " I'll tell you my opinion. All your life you've done exactly what you wanted. The rest of us have been too dumb or too scared."

Usher gauged the distance to the bar. The men sitting there had their backs turned. Beyond them, white-jacketed waiters were immobile in front of the mirrored bottles. He pitched his voice to carry across the table and no farther.

" You sound exactly like a jailhouse psychiatrist, Jamie. Don't you think I *know* where a thief finishes—in a charity ward or the gutter. A thief's like a fighter. He's got just so many earning years ahead of him. It's only a matter of time before his legs go—then his wind. His brain quits last of all. And still he keeps at it. Sooner or later, all he wants to do is to lie down and stop taking punishment. By then it's too late. I don't figure the way I've lived is particularly smart. If they gave me a replay I might even astonish you. As it is, I'm cutting my losses. The best way I know. The *only* way."

Scott was listening, his lean face serious. Now he leaned forward, his eyes friendly.

" You don't have to convince me, Craig. Could I ask you one thing—something about this set-up that bothers me?"

Usher heard his own voice shape its answer. " Go ahead."

" It's the girl," said Scott.

Usher hooked the slice of lemon from his glass. He took his time about wiping his fingers on his handkerchief.

" Caroline. What about her?"

Scott's warmth took the edge off his criticism. " We've exhausted the moral indignation bit, Craig. I meant what I said—I'm in this with you now as deep as I can go. But you set this kid up. I'm entitled to know how you're going to deal with her when it's all over."

71

Usher chose his words carefully. "Get this straight. In the first place, I set up *nobody*. In the second place, what I do with her is none of your business."

Scott slid down on his shoulder-blades, crossed his legs and stared at the ceiling.

"God Almighty, you're thin-skinned. And you talk about me having a chip! All I'm trying to say is that Chestnut Gate'll hold you and me—it won't hold your girl-friends. Let's talk about something more profitable. Epsom Downs cover a lot of territory. How can you be sure where you'll find Balaban?"

Usher's irritation died. They were acting like a couple of kids who'd hooked the same fish. He broke the deadlock gladly.

"Because I've been down there four times and watched his routine. It never varies. He drives in by the road across the racetrack—parks on the edge of the gallop and just sits there with a pair of binoculars. If he gets out, it's to walk a dozen yards—no more. Then he goes back to the car. He's got a heart condition and carries too much weight."

Scott scowled at the end of his cigarette. His objection was considered. "A trainer's bound to have a word with his owner. What about Matt Fogarty?"

Usher pulled his finger across his gullet. "He's had Balaban up to here. The last couple of times, Fogarty's ridden up to the Downs on an animal that would split you wide open. Balaban doesn't go within a quarter-mile of him."

Scott hung his next question in the air as delicately as a spider-thread. "What about this Belgian—he's going to see I'm green. Are you sure he's all right?"

He signalled the offer of a refill. Usher refused.

"Van der Pouk's always been on the level. He's shrewd and the people behind him don't play around. All you have to do is deliver the loot on time. I've given Van der Pouk a price for what we're certain will be in the safe. If there's a dividend—if you find more than we expected—he'll make you an offer. Take it. His figure will be twenty per cent better than we'd get anywhere else."

Scott rapped a couple of smokes from the blue pack. Something was still troubling him. His tone was dubious.

"You mean thirty thousand pounds change hands just like that?"

Usher watched the nicotine staining his finger as he held the cigarette. "Just like that. The quickest, safest, most final way of doing business in the world—selling to a reliable buyer. You're dealing with pros, Jamie. It's better than a contract signed in a lawyer's office."

Van der Pouk arrived as the clock-hand nicked the half-hour. He stood in the doorway, locating the two men in the corner. He showed no sign of recognition until he had inspected the entire room. He bought his own glass of wine at the bar and carried it over. There were no introductions. Nothing except Usher's blunt demand.

"What about the money—did you get that fixed?"

Van der Pouk regarded the backs of his fingers with interest. The skin between knuckles was thatched with soft, dark hair.

"I told you I would have to consult my friends. They are uneasy, Craig."

Usher had lied in the Belgian's office. From the beginning, Van der Pouk had been an integral part of the scheme. With a haul of this size, there *was* nowhere else Usher could go. The risk was too great. A guy like Simey Nussbaum could find the money but Simey had stayed in business for twenty years by feeding the cops an odd victim. He had as many arrests to his credit as a rookie cop hungry for promotion. Anyone who dabbled with Nussbaum took the chance of being high or low man on the totem pole.

Usher's voice hardened. "What the hell are they uneasy about?"

Van der Pouk lipped his drink fastidiously and set it down. He spread his hands wide.

73

"I warned you how it might be. They want to be sure that the goods exist. That's all."

Usher's jaw muscles tightened till they hurt. "I've never tried to pull anything on you, Jean. You could have told them that."

Van der Pouk's massive head brooded. He looked up, his smile displaying the artistry of gold inlaywork.

"I did. They asked me if thirty thousand pounds had ever been at stake. You must be reasonable, Craig. It is a simple question of good faith. Just tell me the source of your supply—that will be enough. To-morrow I shall come wherever you wish with the money. In Swiss francs. Used, thousand-franc notes."

Scott's fingers were turning the ash-tray endlessly. Usher sensed his cousin's uneasiness. The Belgian's wheeling and dealing could only sap Scott's newfound confidence. Usher was genuinely puzzled. By to-morrow afternoon, every corner newsboy would be bawling the details of the robbery. But for some reason the people behind the Belgian wanted to know the source now.

"All I asked you was if you had the money," Usher reminded. "Not where it came from. You're making the deal impossible. We're wasting our time," he told Scott curtly. "Let's move." He started to rise from his seat.

Van der Pouk's short arms barred their exit. He used his hands like an orchestra leader coaxing restraint from the woodwind.

"Do not be hasty, Craig. I tell you, this demand is not mine. I am not alone. But there *is* an alternative."

Usher lowered himself back in his seat. At a push, he could break up the stuff himself. Jamie could hop a plane with a pocketful of loose diamonds. Switzerland was the place. Zurich or Geneva. If they worked fast, they could have the stones sold before the police there were notified. The thought gave his voice an edge of independence.

"What sort of alternative?"

Van der Pouk hitched his chair forward, drawing them to fresh intimacy.

" Only one of you will come to the rendezvous. I shall be accompanied."

Less the words than the manner of their delivery gave Usher the clue. This was the real fear in the Belgian's mind. A meeting in some deserted spot promoted by a false-pretence sale. A rendezvous where Van der Pouk was either slugged or shot and the money taken from him.

Usher's grin was derisive. " A simple matter of good faith."

The gold glinted again in Van der Pouk's mouth.

" Precaution, if you prefer."

" Be as many as you like, Jean," Usher answered quietly. " How much time will you need in the morning—have you done anything about an airplane ticket?"

The Belgian was politely evasive. " I am not yet certain of my plans. It is better that you make the arrangements you think necessary. Where must I bring the money?"

Usher's glance slid to Scott. His cousin's eyebrows were dragged together. He was still fiddling with the ash-tray.

Usher spoke quietly. " Hyde Park. There's a bridge over the Serpentine by the Armoury. Almost opposite is a space by the trees where you can park. Do you know it?"

The Belgian nodded. " And a path by the side of the lake to the boathouse."

Usher lifted his chin at Scott. " He'll be there between nine-fifteen and nine-thirty. You pay him."

Van der Pouk inspected Scott thoroughly. He gave the impression that, once committed to memory, the picture would never be forgotten.

" So," he said brusquely. " The time is convenient. I have one more question."

" You *always* have one more question," Usher said wearily.

Van der Pouk's barrel chest filled. He held the trapped air fully a minute before exhaling.

" My friends are prudent. A parked car at that hour in the morning might be conspicuous. What if your associate never arrives?"

The lighting where they sat was subdued. It was still bright enough to show the flush creeping into Scott's face. He addressed the Belgian for the first time.

" I can only think of one reason why I wouldn't be there. I hope you've got another."

Van der Pouk's eyes were chestnuts swimming in glycerine. He looked to Usher for understanding, sensing a nuance beyond his command of English.

" He means if there's a change of plan," Usher told Scott. He put the Belgian at ease. " He'll be there."

Van der Pouk climbed on his feet. He smiled carefully for Scott's benefit.

" I drive a grey D.S.; registration number 875 EPB. I am punctual. Good night, gentlemen."

He disassociated himself from the table like a man who had found himself there by accident. In spite of his bulk he moved swiftly. By the time they had settled their bar-bill and reached the Knightsbridge exit there was no sign of him. The doorman whistled up a car. Usher gave a direction and shut the glass partition between them and the driver.

" What got into you back there?" he asked curiously.

Scott was holding his hat on his knees. He pulled down the window, leaning into the rush of cool air from the park.

" I didn't like what he said. I didn't like the way he said it."

Usher shrugged. " Van der Pouk's an odd mixture. In general, I'm suspicious of these Resistance heroes. Half of the time, their antics didn't go beyond chalking rude words on walls at dead of night. Or cutting off some whore's hair for fraternising. Van der Pouk was a much tougher proposition. Don't let that suave-Continental routine throw you. Two things are certain to-morrow. Whoever's with him will be armed—and we'll get our money."

Scott said nothing.

" You haven't asked where we're going," Usher said curiously.

Scott shut his window and leaned back. " I'm learning not to ask questions."

The cab cut north at Prince's Gate lights. It passed the forlorn and shuttered tea-gardens and crossed the bridge over the sliver of lake. Usher pointed at the black-topped parking space, as deserted now as it would be at nine in the morning.

" That's where you meet Van der Pouk. You'll be driving Balaban's car. We're going to his home now. I want to be sure you can handle it."

Scott accepted the news as if the destination were the only rational one. His comment was brief.

" At this stage of the game, what's another burglary?" The dimmed headlamps of an oncoming car revealed the nervousness of his mouth.

Usher looked away quickly, staring at the shadows beyond the trees.

" Do you still feel you're being dragged into this, Jamie?"

The cab lurched east into the Bayswater Road. Scott retrieved his hat from the floor. His voice was flat and hard.

" To-morrow's a long way off for me. What say you take me as I am till then?"

They stood in the quiet of Hampstead, waiting till the tail-lights of the cab disappeared. The avenue dropped sharply, luminous under street lamps hidden among the beeches along the pavements. On the other side of the walled gardens, the houses were remote and isolated. The expanse of heath above, the stillness undisturbed by traffic, gave a pastoral quality to the scene. A dying bonfire left a faint smell of woodsmoke that completed the illusion.

They climbed the hill, past red-brick walls and painted

gates and turned into a dead-end. A wattle fence topped with wire netting blocked the impasse. A gate in it was fastened by a padlock. Usher undid the screws holding one of the staples. The padlock dangled uselessly. He pushed his cousin through to the tennis courts. The white marking lines glimmered in the half-light. They ran across and shinned the wall behind the shingle clubhouse. They dropped, ankle-deep in leaves. Usher led the way, using the trees as cover. They had flanked the modern brick house facing the avenue and now stood directly behind it. Light from a window touched the lawn where they stood— illuminated the yard between house and garage. They inched forward, their eyes on the uniformed maid standing in front of the window. When they were immediately in front of the kitchen door, Usher signalled. They ducked below the level of the woman's view and ran silently round the yard to the garage. The weighted entrance flap was suspended above their heads. They groped into the darkness, stumbling against the fender of the heavy town car. The radiator was still warm. The coachbuilt door opened easily under Usher's hand. A light came on in the roof, showing the ignition keys hanging on the dashboard.

Scott was leaning against the side of the car. His hat was pulled down tight about his ears.

" It's a Mark Ten Jaguar—non automatic, with an ordinary four-speed gearbox."

Usher took a deep breath. Everything he did the other seemed to construe as a challenge.

" Then get behind the wheel and show me," he said in a whisper.

Scott obeyed. The motor switched off, he flicked the gear shift through its changes. He touched one control after another with gloved fingers.

" Lights, horn, starter. O.K. ?" The two men looked at one another, strained and unsmiling. " O.K. ?" Scott repeated.

Usher nodded. Jamie wasn't being dragged. He was flogging himself to be out front. They closed the car and left the shelter of the garage. A box-hedge and herbaceous border swept round to the front of the house. A light hung over the blue door at the top of the steps. The long, well-proportioned windows facing them had deep sills set at chest level. Indigo curtains were drawn in the room on the right, insulating its warmth and comfort.

Usher distributed his weight firmly on the gravel. A narrow runway circled the house between flower-beds and walls. The two men jumped down on the blind side of the steps, edging under the stone arch to the lighted window. A woman's voice called inside. The man's answer came muffled and unclear. Usher stood flat against the brickwork. He sidled nearer the chink in the curtain. A middle-aged woman sat on the sofa, her feet propped on a tapestry stool. She was small and round, like a plump pigeon. She was holding out the sock she was darning for inspection. The fat man in front of the fire was smiling. His heavy body bulged from a velvet smoking jacket. The most dominant thing about his face was the nose. A soaring structure of bone, untouched by the flesh droops and curves that surrounded it. The hair on his head was the colour and texture of unspun cotton.

Usher's pulse accelerated. The God's-eye view always excited him. This couple imagined themselves completely entrenched in privacy—secured against intrusion by a screen of brick and glass. A telephone call would bring police cars racing to their aid. He caught Scott by the sleeve, urging him forward to share the picture.

"Balaban," he mouthed. Scott pulled away hurriedly. They retreated from the window to the shelter of the shrubbery. They used the same route for their return. They waited in the dead-end, outside the tennis-courts, brushing their clothes and shoes free of dirt. When they were done, they walked back down the hill, matching strides. Scott's hat was back at a normal angle. His head was down as if he were counting the cracks in the pavement. His voice was concerned.

"A world-famous jeweller disappears. It's established that someone clears out his safe but there's no sign how it's been done. Doesn't Interpol come in on a thing like that?"

Usher was startled. The remark was completely unexpected. "What put a thing like that into your head?"

A bus lumbered by at the foot of the hill. They were nearing the bustle of the Finchley Road.

"I read the newspapers," Scott said doggedly.

Usher came to a dead halt. "You read the newspapers!" he said scathingly. "Next thing you'll tell me you watch television. Interpol agents getting on and off jet airplanes—loaded down with handcuffs and geiger counters. Do you want to know just what Interpol is—the biggest bluff since the Maginot line! A dozen crummy little offices where civilians pull files. Clearing houses for information. There isn't a guy in any of them with the power of arrest. You might as well worry about the Wasauga Watch Committee as Interpol."

Scott grinned. "You've made your point."

The cab dropped them off at the corner of Old Compton Street. Neon signs jumped over the coffee mills and spaghetti parlours, the near-beer joints and cellar clubs. The blare of half a dozen bands combined with the clatter of passing exhausts. Beyond red velvet curtains, waiters stood against gold walls like wax dummies. Soho glittered for the negroes, grey-faced with cold—the self-conscious provincials on their way to the strip-tease theatres—the dark, neat men who waited in watchful groups at the intersections.

Usher turned up Dean Street. Two women beckoned from a doorway. Inside, someone was banging out standards on an off-key piano. The blonde plucked at Usher's elbow, her eyes bored but her voice inviting.

"Are you boys looking for a little fun?"

He swatted away the hand as he might have done a fly. "Save your breath. There's no action here."

Fifty yards on, he led the way into a badly-lit courtyard. Barred dirty windows flanked the walk-up entrance. A few cards were tacked against the side of the open door. Their text was either blatant or improbable.

MARK SPENCER EXPORT-IMPORT
(LONDON, PARIS, NEW YORK)

SWAMI RAMACHAND
HOROSCOPES READ
TAP THE UNERRING WISDOM OF THE EAST

KIKI DE LA TORRE
(40 - 28 - 40)
FRENCH LESSON GIVEN BY APPOINTMENT
*(Third Floor — Two Rings)*

The last sign had been splash-painted by an amateur.

THE SAD SACK SOCIAL CLUB
MEMBERS ONLY

Usher stopped at the foot of the dirty staircase. " We're going to have one drink in this dump. Whatever I say, you go along with it."

Scott shrugged. " You know me."

They climbed through stale air to the lighted second floor. Usher pushed the door in front of them. The room was empty but for a couple of whores drinking gin, an elderly drunk asleep with his head on the counter. The barman looked up. Every visible inch of his skin was covered with tattoo work. A Chinese dragon writhed on his shaven skull, its front claws and mouth descending to his forehead. Concentric whorls decorated his cheeks and neck while the backs of his hands and fingers were indigo birds. He wore a fine wool shirt and no jacket. Recognising Usher, he showed stained teeth in a guarded smile.

"If it isn't my old mate, Dasher!" He came to the end of the bar, arms outstretched like a priest invoking sacrifice. He dropped the pose suddenly, small ferocious eyes regarding Scott. "One of ours, is he?" he asked knowingly.

Usher's manner was easy. "Mr. Green's a journalist, Waxey. He's doing a piece on prisons. I thought you two ought to meet."

The barman slid the Members' Book along the counter. "Sign 'im in, Dasher. We got these snotty-nosed cops coming in all hours, looking for trouble. A journalist!" The thought seemed to fascinate him.

Usher ordered a couple of drinks. "And no Uncle Tom Cobley Scotch, Waxey. Pour from the right bottle."

The bartender's tattooed face twisted with pleasure as if he had been paid a compliment. He polished the insides of the two glasses fastidiously. He was still considering Scott's appearance minutely. He was near enough for the onion on his breath to be apparent.

"Show the bastards up mate!" he burst out suddenly. "That's what you got to do—give the public the truth." "Truth" became "trewf," delivered in a dying whistle.

"That's exactly what Mr. Green wants to do," Usher turned to Scott. "Mr. Wax and I were inside together. In fact we were neighbours in the Punishment Cells."

The barman frowned, the dragon on his scalp moving with the intensity of his emotion. Usher went on. "We were unlucky enough to fall foul of the Landing Screw. He bagged us both. My crime was lending Mr. Wax a library book. His, borrowing it."

The two whores had turned in their seats, their expressions carefully composed to sympathy. The elderly drunk slept on. The room waited for Usher to continue. He pushed his fingers through his white shock, talking as if the recollection were no more than mildly amusing. "It should have stopped there—but the Governor took a dislike to both of us. With me it was mutual. Mr. Wax was guilty of Dumb Insolence. The strong-arm squad threw him down a flight of iron stairs and broke three of his ribs. When he came out of hospital he took a swing at one of them and finished in front of the Visiting Magistrates. Mr. Wax had his back scratched. Show him, Waxey."

The barman turned swiftly, taking off the woollen shirt with practised readiness. The flesh from shoulder-blades to kidneys was crisscrossed with fine white scars. Usher saw the repugnance in his cousin's eyes and made his voice hard again.

"Mr. Wax remembers what they say. 'We'll keep a cell for you!' They like you to fight—it whets their appetite. Then they can kill you a little bit each day."

The bartender's face was anxious—like a dog that seeks to understand a new and unfamiliar command. Usher laid a bill on the counter. "Put your shirt on," he said quietly—"So long, Waxey. Mr. Green will see that it gets in the paper." He bared his teeth at the whores and walked out.

Down in the courtyard, he stopped to light a cigarette. Scott's expression was quizzical under the lamp.

"What was all that in aid of? I never imagined jails to be kindergartens."

Usher looked up at the club windows. "I don't have to tell you—Waxey's not bright. He wouldn't have gotten by the first paragraph of the book I lent him. But it represented the difference between oblivion and the sordidness of what we were living. For that he finished with his back like a raw hamburger. It was on our way home, anyway. I wanted you to know why I'd never go inside again, Jamie. That's all." He buttoned his coat, his voice careless.

It was almost eight when they reached the gloomy square off the Earl's Court Road. Scott stood beneath the peeling portico, viewing the filthy steps with distaste. Usher opened the street door. The hallway was redolent with the smell of brussels sprouts cooking. A row of cats sat sphinx-like outside the door at the bottom of the stairs to the basement.

Usher grinned. Scott was going to see how the poor really lived.

"Second-floor back and mind the milk bottles," he invited.

A pile of unclaimed letters lay on the marble-topped hall-stand. Bills, income-tax demands, wafer-thin envelopes bearing exotic stamps. On the baize board over the table was a note in Mrs. Sangster's handwriting. Usher pulled it out.

*Miss Woodall telephoned twice. Will you please ring her at home as soon as you come in? E.S.*

He had a flush of uneasiness. The pay-phone was lodged on the second story. An extension served the upper part of the house. Caroline rarely called him here. She had an aversion to sharing her conversation with eavesdroppers. He stuffed the piece of paper in his pocket without comment.

Upstairs, a light showed under Mrs. Sangster's door. He opened his own room and locked it behind them. He drew the thin curtains. The fireplace had long since been bricked-in. He dropped a coin in the meter, exploding a match in the broken burners of the gas fire.

"Keep your voice down," he told Scott. "We're all interested in one another's business here."

Scott threw his hat on the bed and took the only chair. He seemed to have acquired fresh poise. He watched Usher unwrap the cardboard box like a man at someone else's birthday party—about to be shown a gift in which he must display interest. Usher cut the string and emptied the package on to the bed. The two suits of overalls were of heavy blue twill with battledress tops. Ex-Civil Defence issue that he had bought at a Government Surplus store off the Charing Cross Road. He ripped out each identifying label and burnt them in the flame of the gas fire. The tired bed-springs sagged under his weight. He pulled one of the battledress suits over his own clothing. The wrists and ankles were elasticised. The front zipped high to the throat. He broke the seal on a cellophane wrapper and pushed the toe of one nylon stocking into the other. He dragged the flimsy mesh over his head and tucked the ends of the stockings into his neckline. His features were formless under the double thickness. He topped the outfit with a blue beret.

Scott watched the performance with interest. The in-out thud of the rowing machine started up across the landing. He half-turned towards the sound and then relaxed.

"What's the idea of two stockings—I thought you used one?"

"Nylons snag," said Usher. "The second's insurance."

He stripped himself of the camouflage and packed the two outfits back in their box. "I've got to find my way to Epsom. I can't risk a cab at that time in the morning. That leaves the train or bus. Whichever I use, there'll be someone aboard who'd remember a man carrying a box. You can take this stuff home—bring it with you to-morrow."

Scott nodded. He leaned forward, stretching out a hand to the hissing blue flames of the gas stove.

"Let's go over it one more time. I bring nothing in the horsebox but a headstall and a hay-net. If I'm stopped for any reason at all, I'm on my way to the sales to look for a likely animal. Whatever happens I stick to this story. I time myself to reach Epsom at six-thirty. You'll be there, waiting in front of the Downs Hotel."

Usher interrupted quickly. "Like hell I will—not in front. Nobody must see you pick me up. When you reach the hotel, keep going until you come to a cut-off on your left. There's a haybarn just behind the hedge—you can't miss it. Get out and take a look at your tyres. If the road's clear, you'll see me. If it isn't, turn up the cut-off and stop. I won't be far away."

He started to pace from the window—five steps forward, five steps back. He whistled tonelessly as he walked.

85

Scott waited for a couple of minutes then sat up very straight. His voice was still quiet but passionate.

" For Christ's sake, can't you cut out that patrol, Craig! And all the time with the bloody whistle. It's getting on my nerves."

The outburst stopped Usher in his tracks. He was only vaguely conscious of a habit that took him the length of a cell and back. He pulled himself from the memory.

" We both need sleep—and you've got a journey ahead of you."

Scott collected the box from the end of the bed. His loss of control had been momentary. The beginning of a grin lifted the corners of his mouth.

" Sleep, the man says—are you kidding! If you need me, I'll be home by eleven."

Usher unlocked the door, opening it no more than inches. The geyser was roaring on the next floor. Someone was banging around in the bathroom. He beckoned Scott to follow. They tiptoed down the stairs. Usher waited till the sound of his cousin's footsteps died outside. Then he slipped through the street door, hurrying towards the telephone booths in the subway station.

Caroline's number was engaged. He kept dialling till he obtained an answer. Her voice sounded relieved.

" Craig—my goodness, what a man to track down! Where on earth have you been?"

He spoke guardedly. "Out. I told you I had to see about that job. I've been with the guy till now. What was it you wanted?"

Her laugh was a mixture of affection and irritation.

" You know, darling, I wouldn't say you sounded wildly enthusiastic. And here am I telling Mr. Balaban all about my admirer—I was talking to him about you to-day."

His heart leapt and died. The receiver dropped in his hand, her tinny voice remote and insistent.

" Are you there, Craig?"

He wet his lips and answered. " I'm here."

She gave him the news eagerly. " We were talking horses. I told him I knew this man who was interested. He's driving me down with him to-morrow morning. If you'd like to come, you have an invitation."

His thoughts ran too fast for reason. Instinct prompted a flat negative. But he hedged.

" I can't make it to-morrow. Look—why don't we wait till later in the week—then we can go together."

Her answer echoed in the recesses of his mind. " That's no good either. To-morrow's the last day he's going down to watch exercises. I think he's finally realised he's overdone it with Fogarty. Can't you possibly manage it, Craig? —we'll be back by nine."

He was still struggling with a sense of violent upheaval. He could only manage a semblance of his usual manner towards her. Caution told him that his excuse had to tie in with the alibi he had prepared.

" I haven't been sleeping, honey. I thought I'd take a bomb to-night—get a good night's rest. I've got another interview to-morrow. Tell Mr. Balaban thanks for the offer. I'll call you as soon as you get back from work to-morrow night. O.K.?"

He waited anxiously for her reply. It held no trace of suspicion.

" O.K. But I don't like to think of you taking pills—it's not you. Good night, darling, and good luck to-morrow."

He walked away from the subway station and lost himself in the shadows of the square. He was unwilling to face the confines of the house until he'd had time to reflect.

Always the unknown factor sought to destroy him. This time it was human instead of mechanical. There was too much at stake to turn back—to work out a new plan for grabbing Balaban. Any suggestion of delay or compromise would cool Jamie or Van der Pouk—maybe both of them. He'd be left in that stinking room, alone and penniless, to start all over again. There *was* no alternative. They'd have to treat Caroline in the same way as the jeweller. She was young, resilient. In a little while she'd forget the experience. In the months to come, even laugh about it. If Jamie's sensibilities took a jolt, too bad. The slightest slip now and they were both finished. Only the thickness of a pair of stockings, the clothing he'd bought, would disguise him from a girl who knew the very soles of his feet. They'd have to work fast and in complete silence. Somehow he had to camouflage his appearance still further, to leave an impression of physical characteristics strong enough to baffle a woman's intuition.

A car door slammed across the square. A girl's voice was adamant in farewell. It was getting late. He made his way round to the house and climbed the stairs to his landing.

The light was still on behind Mrs. Sangster's door. He tapped softly on the panel. The voice inside was startled.

" Who is it?"

He put his mouth to the crack, speaking softly. " It's me —Craig Usher."

" Just a minute, I'll open the door." The key was turned and a bolt withdrawn. Mrs. Sangster looked out uncertainly. She was wearing her wrapper. Her faded hair was confined in a net and her face shone with some sort of grease.

He smiled apology. " I'm sorry if I disturbed you—it's about the milk in the morning. I'm taking a pill. I hope I'll be sleeping late. I thought I'd let you know."

She moved towards him, caught in sudden confidence. " What sign are you?"

" Sign?" he repeated. " Oh that! God knows. Leo, I think."

She nodded mysteriously. " That's what I suspected. You've still got the winter to get through. You must keep your feet dry. I'll leave your milk outside your door. Good night, Mr. Usher." She waited, giving him light to unlock his own room, fluttered her fingers and disappeared.

He sat on the side of the bed. He'd be out before anyone

stirred in the morning. Later, there was a dead period in the house between eleven and twelve. All the tenants left for either school or office. He could slip back into his room unobserved when the old bag in the basement did her shopping. He'd get Jamie to telephone the house about noon. Mrs. Ellis would answer and call him. He could make a production about oversleeping. Three women would be ready to say he hadn't stirred since the night before. No contrived alibi could be foolproof but this one would never be put to the test.

He rose on sudden impulse and unfastened the scarred rawhide suitcase. Hidden under a pile of clothing was a .45 automatic. He pulled the breech back and tested the firing mechanism. The trigger-release was still. He worked a little olive oil into the spring and bar. He found the clip of shells. They were still heavy with their original film of grease. He loaded the weapon and screwed the silencer into the barrel.

It was eighteen years since he'd fired one of the things. The trick was that what the army taught you was never forgotten.

*Now to aim—think of the barrel as an extension of your forefinger. Don't jerk when you fire—squeeze the trigger gently. And count your shots—you might have one less than you think.*

He put the gun out of sight on the dressing-table and set the alarm-clock for five. When he had washed his face and teeth he cut out the light. He fell asleep hearing Caroline's voice as it had been an hour ago—warm and enthusiastic with her news.

# JAMES SCOTT

He came downstairs, for some reason carrying his shoes like
an interloper. The steady thumping of the wolfhound's tail
greeted him in the warm kitchen. He peered through the
curtains. It was still night. A nebulous moon tipped in a
ragged sky. Snowflakes, like white moths, sailed across the
yard to liquidate themselves against the heat of the window-
pane. He eased on his shoes and fixed himself a little food.
The wedge of bread, butter and banana made a buffer that
would stop the walls of his stomach grinding together. He
re-heated last night's coffee and added a slug of Scotch.
Then he sat at the table, forcing himself to eat and drink.
On the other side of the room, the hound lay stretched like
a lion, tawny head between its forepaws, yellow eyes vigil-
ant.

A sporting calendar was pinned against the dresser. The
thirty-first of the month had been ringed in pencil. The
Internal Revenue's last day of grace, he remembered. His
mouth full but without saliva, he rose and tore December
from the pad. He crumpled the slip of paper in his hand.
January would be just another year—it *must* be another
existence. He wrote a note and propped it against the
percolator.

*Have gone to sales—back this afternoon. J.S.*

Parrish who knew as well as any just how broke the place
was would think he'd gone crazy. The clock in the living-
room chimed five. Time he went. He cleared the table reluctantly and fired the stove. He moved slowly, as if each
gesture made relinquished his hold on security. He thought
a little about that, reminding himself on what his salvation

90

depended. This time there could be no thought of failure. Craig had been positive and Craig's load was as heavy as his own. One thing was sure—Saturday night had blooded him. He was no longer a beginner. He remembered the dropping elevator with excitement rather than fear. He opened the kitchen door, calling the dog after him.

The trailer was already attached to the Land-Rover. He threw the box with the battledress underneath the front seat and rechecked every detail for the third time since his return. The fuel tank wouldn't hold another pint. The tyre-pressures were accurate. The safety-catch on the hitch operated properly. He buttoned his coat against the weather. As if sensing Scott's mood, the hound wet the wall and settled in the straw beneath the barn, resigned and reproachful. A horse stirred in its stable across the yard.

Scott hit the starter. The trailer swung behind, jolting into the familiar chuckholes along the avenue. He followed the curving wall of the vicarage. Another hour and Mathieson would be kneeling alone in his church, praying for the souls of his parish—Scott's included. " The mirror of the soul," as he described it unoriginally. Scott thought that by that reasoning his own conscience was likely to be troublesome before the day was over. But he doubted it.

Only a rooster challenged the silence of the village. Scott's headlamps swept the short street, reflected in the curtained windows. Once round the bend by the sawmill, he accelerated past the gates guarding Lallie Mellor's empty house. The scene with her husband was far from forgotten. Just as the stink of failure had alienated everyone in the bar, news of his solvency would spread in the neighbourhood. Not that he cared. If Craig and he had a few decent horses, a little luck in their running—the right to open the morning's mail without a churning gut—that was all he asked. The sort of life they wanted demanded no more for its fulfilment. Craig's installation at Chestnut Gate was already accepted in Scott's thinking. The Mellors and their customers—the stockbroking landowners and their ginned-up wives—would have something to talk about other than the iniquity of supertax. Craig's arrival would explain everything neatly for them. It was made to order. The cousin from Canada with money—who didn't blow his nose on his fingers—and was therefore respectable. A gentleman, in fact, and unattached. With any sort of luck, Craig's peculiar brand of respectability would jolt the local marriageable daughters into shocked discomfiture. And Caroline Woodall . . . for a guy who had played the field for twenty years, Craig's touchiness on the subject was abnormal. Maybe he too had a conscience.

Basingstoke was a wilderness of damp, empty streets. A fat steamer of smoke from the drowsing brewery added its mite to the lowering cloud now obscuring the moon. The snow skated in thin flurries, too sparse to hold the ground. Surely not enough to stop a tough Irish trainer from exercising his string. He put the thought out of mind determinedly. There was little traffic on the A3. Now and again he answered the friendly flash of a long-distance truck. Eight miles on, he turned east again. A quarter of an hour took him to the foot of Epsom Downs. He pulled on to the shoulder of the road and checked his watch. Six-twenty. The grandstands at the top of the hill were stark and void—useless except for a few days a year. Beyond the nearby hedges and garden walls, a few lighted windows patched the fronts of suburban villas. A milk-wagon rattled along a nearby lane.

He looked up at the sky anxiously, filled with quick foreboding. The snow had completely stopped. There was no wind. But the burgeoning clouds, the chill air, had the hush that presaged a heavy fall. He pitched his cigarette-butt at the grass verge. A blackbird rose, melodious in alarm. He put the Land-Rover in low gear and crawled up the incline. Day was breaking fast over the downland. He cut his headlamps, easing momentum as he neared the hotel. A hayrick ahead marked the cut-off. He braked short of the junction and jumped down to the road. It was clear in both directions. There was no sign of Usher.

Scott fumbled half-heartedly with the trailer hitch. Maybe Craig had called off the deal. He could well have phoned after five-thirty. Scott had a picture of the bell ringing in the empty room—the dog's answering rumble from the yard outside. He slammed down the safety-catch on the hitch, hearing the noise behind the hedge. Someone was forcing his way through the thick hawthorn. Usher appeared, using his back as a buffer, protecting his head with his arms. Scott jumped into the cab, opened the off-side door and switched on the ignition. The motor's clatter was an affront to the hushed fields.

Usher's piebald head was hatless. A razor scrape had dried angrily in the cleft of his chin. He jerked his head impatiently.

" Roll—there's no time to waste."

He piloted the way past the empty paddocks and grand-stands. He peered through the windshield, pointing to the left.

" Pull over by the gate—close to the wall."

Scott manœuvred his cargo into a position out of sight of the road. He followed his cousin to the gate in the railings. Usher fitted a heavy key in the lock. They sprinted across snow-sodden turf to the rear of the shuttered totalisator windows. Sheltered in an angle were three telephone booths. Usher pulled one door after another, staying long enough in each to test the instrument for a dialling tone. He scribbled three sets of numbers on a piece of paper, omitting the exchange. He gave the slip to Scott.

" You read these from right to left, backwards. As soon as you're through with Van der Pouk, ring any one of these numbers. I'll be waiting here from nine o'clock on."

Scott signalled assent. Usher's curt confidence took him back twenty years to a Bomber Command airfield. The clanking steam-pipes, the encumbrance of the flying-suit, the faces of the men on the benches beside him—attentive

93

to the briefing from the end of the room. Then, too, every probability had been checked. Flak, weather and fighter opposition. All of it to be forgotten the moment the bomb-ports opened. Survival then became an act of faith and not of reason.

" I'll call the moment I'm through," he promised.

Usher's eyes looked as though he had slept for a month. But he lowered them and swung his head in a tired way.

" You may as well know now, Jamie. We've got two of them to deal with. Balaban's bringing the girl." He turned away before Scott could answer.

They trotted back to the gate. Usher relocked it carefully. They sat in the warmth of the cab, carefully avoiding one another's look. Scott marvelled at the calmness of his own voice. " The disguise won't fool her. She *has* to recognise you, Craig."

Usher revealed the heavy automatic in his lap. He weighed it in his open palm. " *This* is what she'll recognise," he said grimly.

The shape of the silencer fascinated Scott. In some strange way he found acceptance of the weapon no more difficult than the rest of it. The rules were Craig's—the gun a symbol of his authority.

" What happened—about the girl, I mean?"

Usher looked at himself hard in the mirror, picking the flecked blood from his chin.

" They'll do it every time. She talked herself into the trip and had me invited. There's no alternative—Balaban's not coming down any more." He turned from his reflection to check his watch. " Let's go."

They bumped through a gap in the rails bordering the track. Across the vast infield, they swung left away from Tattenham Corner and mounted the slope. Here, Usher undid his door, guiding Scott over the sand-track and through a break in the undergrowth. A faint, angry light flared over the far Kentish hills. The ground dipped sharply on all sides, traversed by sheeptracks and bridlepaths.

Usher took the wheel, ramming the square snout of the Land-Rover through the gorse and bramble. He stopped in a clearing barely large enough to contain the two vehicles. The convoy was in a circle of dense bush, completely hidden from the gallops.

Usher started to rip the cover from the cardboard box. He distributed the clothing, talking in short snatches as he dressed.

"Don't let the gun bother you—there's going to be no shooting."

Scott was struggling into his battledress top. The nylon stockings masked Usher's features. He pulled the beret low on his ears. A grotesque hump bulged between his shoulders. He emptied a paper sack on the seat beside him. Lint pads and wadded cotton, an outsize roll of surgical tape.

The mesh over Scott's face allowed complete vision. He felt it suck into his mouth as he spoke. "I'm fit. Just tell me what I have to do."

Usher tucked the automatic into his tunic. "We've *got* to swing this, Jamie. Thank Christ the snow's held off. I'll get them out of the car. As soon as they're in the bushes, I'll help you tape them up. Whatever happens, they mustn't see the horsebox. Do a good job on them. And don't open your mouth—not even to cough."

He waited with cocked head, listening to the faint drumming from the bottom of the hill. "That's the first lot of horses. They'll be up in ten minutes. Balaban ought to show any moment."

Scott was glad that his face was screened. His stomach felt as though he hadn't eaten. He did his best to sound casual.

"Is that gun loaded?"

Usher opened his door. "Next question," he said indifferently.

The raised ramp formed the back of the horsebox. A small wicket in the side gave access to the front. A shoulder-high partition divided the space inside. A head-collar and hay-net hung where a groom usually stood. Usher's inspection was hurried. " Couldn't be better. Like this we can put one on either side." He wheeled at the sound of a motor and ran into the gorse. A car was crossing the gallops towards them. He grabbed the cotton pads he had taped ready and thrust them at Scott. The gun was in his gloved hand.

" Remember—not a word !"

They ran low—behind the screen of bushes, moving parallel with the mounting car. It stopped fifteen yards away. The man and the girl inside were plainly visible. Balaban loomed round the front of the Jaguar. His long overcoat, round fur hat and binoculars, gave him the appearance of a Balkan bandit. He said something to the girl—positioned her so that she faced the ascent that the horses must negotiate. Balaban trained his race-glasses on the bottom of the hill. The naked eye could just distinguish the moving string of horses.

Usher shambled out of the undergrowth, bent and deformed. He was within touching distance of them when they whirled simultaneously. The automatic swung from one to the other like a cobra preparing to strike. Usher motioned with his free hand at the bushes behind them.

Balaban's lips had gone the same colour as his drooping cheeks. The whole of his body seemed frozen in a pose that half-turned him towards his assailant. Gradually his arms lowered, as though the weight of the binoculars had become intolerable. Caroline Woodall screamed once before covering her lips with her hand. Balaban took her elbow gently. He led her into the gorse as if he already knew and accepted the sequel.

Scott sprang from a crouch. Stepping round behind Balaban, he pulled the cotton pad over the jeweller's face. He taped it firmly across the mouth—repeated the manœuvre, using the second pad as a blindfold. Caroline's eyes were on Scott—not Usher. She kicked out wildly as he reached for her. Usher trapped her flailing arms, held her as Scott gagged and blindfolded her. The two figures stumbled forward awkwardly, impelled by their captors.

Scott wrapped both arms round the girl. He lifted her into the trailer like a sack of oats. He fastened her wrists behind her back and pushed her off balance. He caught her legs and tied her ankles. Her whole body shook. She was whimpering softly through the gag. He rolled her on her side and spread a horse-blanket over her.

Outside, Usher had Balaban nailed against the trailer with the barrel of the automatic. The jeweller's trembling arms supported his weight. His head drooped, the binoculars swinging from the strap about his neck. Scott picked the fur hat from the ground. It took both men's efforts to haul Balaban into the horsebox. They dragged him into the empty compartment. Released from their grip, he sagged helplessly. The girl was quiet on the other side of the partition. Usher reached under the jeweller's overcoat, ripping the shirt buttons across the bulging belly. An antelope money-belt was fastened over the soft, white flesh. He undid the buttoned purse with quick fingers. Scott took the double-ended safe key. They used the last of the adhesive tape to secure Balaban's limbs, leaving him comfortable in a cocoon of blanket. They locked the trailer door behind them and jumped up into the Land-Rover.

Both men struggled out of their overalls. The beret and stockings had flattened Usher's badger-brush hair. He turned up a trouser-leg wincing. The skin over his left calf-muscle had been raked by the girl's grinding heel. He dabbed the seeping blood with a handkerchief. He looked up, his eyes triumphant.

" It's all yours, Jamie—we're in business."

Scott made a pile of his discarded clothing. He lodged the safe key deeper in a hip pocket. Beyond the screen of gorse, fifty yards away, horses were thundering up the sand track. Usher straightened the knot in Scott's tie, found his hat for him.

" There'll be nobody near the car. Fogarty makes the

97

lads canter right to the end of the track. It took us just eleven minutes. That's better than I ever hoped for."

Scott's heart banged in his rib-cage. This was less fear than the sick excitement that went with a photo-finish. The race was over. All that remained was to hoist the number into the frame. He threw the next move at Usher, diffident but smiling.

"You'll shift the box, won't you? Once you're on the road, nobody'll give you a second look. There are too many trailers in the area."

Usher nodded. "I'll move off with you—keep rolling till nine o'clock then go to the phone. As soon as you call, I'll take this pair and ditch them. I've got the spot fixed. They'll be safe there for another hour. We'll turn in the alarm ourselves and let the law find them."

"What do I do with the Jaguar?"

"Dump it as soon as you get to Hatton Garden," said Usher. "Use cabs. Be sure you leave the car clean. No prints and no bits of paper. I'll drive the box down to Ascot—leave it outside the station. You can take the train down there. I'll see you at Chestnut Gate to-night."

Scott frowned. "Ascot? I thought you were going to drive the box straight home?"

Usher slid back the catch on his door. "I changed my mind. They see me drive back people in the village ask questions. We've got to play this sales angle all the way. Make sure you're noticed there—make a couple of bids. For all I care, buy something. You'll have the cash."

He came with Scott as far as the gap in the gorse. The whole sky seemed to have lowered, darkening the air so that the stands across the track were almost invisible. One last nimbus of light clung to the brow of the hill. A score of excited horses wheeled in a circle there. A solitary figure sat a hack in the centre. Fogarty would see no more than a parked car driven away.

Usher's hand gripped Scott's. "Do your best, Jamie."

Scott took a deep breath. "You'll be hearing."

He slipped out, head down, using the Jaguar as cover for his approach. The near front door was open. The ignition keys were in the lock. He switched on. Only the flickering gauges betrayed the quiet motor. He wheeled the car across the turf and into the infield. Once on the road behind the grandstands, he braked, looking back at the bottom of the hill. The Land-Rover and trailer were climbing out of the dip, headed for the network of lanes that circled the Downs.

It was a little after eight when he turned into High Holborn. For the last half-hour—ever since the waste of Wimbledon Common—snow had fallen in a determined drive that searched the hidden corners of the city. Already the roofs and window-ledges were powdered. The snow packed gently into the angles of the serried buildings, accentuating the dirtiness of stone and brick façades. A paper-seller was stamping his feet outside the exit to the subway station, his voice chronically hoarse and unintelligible. The benighted few who left the stuffy warmth of the crowded trains stepped carefully through the slush on the sidewalks. Muffled in upturned coat collars, they walked with their eyes on the ground.

Scott drove down Hatton Garden. A hundred yards away, a solitary armoured truck was parked in front of an assay office. The doors at the top of the steps leading to the Wessel Building were open. He wheeled the Jaguar round the first intersection and stopped. The short street was empty. He swivelled the driving mirror and checked his appearance. He remembered the cliché—*Guilt was written all over his face,* sometimes they strengthened the phrase with " indelibly." His unsmiling reflection had the familiarity of a thousand untroubled mornings.

He walked away from the car, stopping to drop the ignition keys down the first gutter-grating. He was obeying Usher's instructions literally without questioning their reason. He turned the corner. The armoured truck was still outside the assay office. He passed it with averted head, hurrying north. Instinct took him beyond the Wessel Building. He loitered for a minute on the pavement at the top of Hatton Garden. He concealed his careful inspection of the street with the mechanics of lighting a cigarette. He was unremarked and alone. He stared briefly towards the pile of the Central Criminal Courts. The Statue of Justice soared above the roofs, blindfold, holding her scales.

The lobby of the Wessel Building was deserted. Its wet marble floor smelled of green soap. An indomitable surge of Cockney song located the bucket brigade far along the corridor. He skirted the damp floor and ran up the stairway. His rubber soles were soundless on the stone treads. At the end of the passage he stopped, facing the door to Balaban's office. His hands were shaking a little but he manipulated both locks without trouble. He turned the handle slowly. In spite of Usher's expertise, Scott half-expected to hear the strident protest of a burglar alarm. He closed the door behind him on a silence almost unbearable.

The light was meagre in the inner room but he dared not risk a lamp. He pulled back the silk screen. Against this solid mass of metal, the double-ended key seemed inadequate. He recreated the scene of the night before, his hand guided by Usher's incisive whisper:

*You make one complete turn to the right—then half a turn back. Like this. The key stays in the lock. You pull the handle down as far as it goes and the safe's open.*

Holding his breath, he pulled. The heavy door swung out, weightless under his grip. A masked bulb came on inside the safe. The interior was smaller than he had expected. Three shelves were placed horizontally, one above the other. The lowest was crowded with flat leather cases. He emptied each container of its contents, piling the jewellery on the carpet at his feet. He returned the cases to the safe and squatted on his haunches. He slipped his wrist through the tiara. The three-pointed coronet sprayed diamonds, the massed facets mocking the dimness of the room with their brilliance. The necklace was an inch-thick choker of square-cut stones, fastened at the back with a solitaire. The ear-rings shivered in a platinum setting, cascades of winking light. Bracelet and ring matched their fellows in beauty and artistry. He wrapped the set carefully in the suède dusters Usher had given him. Only vaguely had he known that such things existed. It seemed incredible that the uncomfortable bundle in his inner breast pocket would be worth all that money.

He thrust his arm deep at the back of the bottom shelf. The haul netted two small packets of loose diamonds in blue tissue paper. These he stuffed into a ticket pocket. It was everything, save for two manila envelopes on the top shelf. He carried them to the window. They were unsealed, the first addressed to a firm of lawyers. He opened the envelope and read the typed document.

To WHOM IT MAY CONCERN, this being the Last Will and Testament of Samuel Gershom Balaban

I, Samuel Gershon Balaban, jewellery maker, residing at The Lawn House, Frognal Reach, Hampstead, in the County of London, do give and bequeath to my wife, Sarah Hannah Balaban, of the above address, the income deriving from shares and investments as listed in the appended memorial to be enjoyed during her lifetime. Furthermore, I give and bequeath to the said Sarah Balaban, all sums of money lodged to my credit in banks here and in Switzerland. These sums shall be used by her as she deems fit.

Upon the decease of my wife, the shares and investments already referred to shall be sold by the executors and the money derived therefrom inherited without restriction by Caroline Andrea Woodall, spinster, residing at 10 Allen Mews, S.W.7, in the County of London.

In the event of the said Caroline Woodall predeceasing the said Sarah Balaban, the estate held in trust shall pass on my wife's death as follows :

101

One half to the trustees of the Middlesex Hospital to apportion as they please.

One half to the committee of the Society for the Encouragement of British Bloodstock to apportion as they please.

A dated and witnessed signature followed. A typewritten list of securities and investments was pinned to the legal document. The second envelope was addressed to Caroline Woodall. The letter inside was dated, fourth of November, 1962. He read on.

Dear Caroline,

No nonsense from an old man who likes living. May it be a long time before you open this. Mrs. Balaban and I have talked a lot about what I'm doing. The children we wanted we never had. When we go, we leave no relatives—not even one whipplesnapper (I put to make you laugh!) to worry how much he should get.

Someday you will marry and raise a family. Choose better a worker, not a loafer. But money you will have, just in case. Because you're a smart girl, you'll ask yourself why does Balaban put me in his will. The answer is simple, dear Caroline. In six months, not a cross word or look—always the smile—a little joke and *goodness*.

By now you know that "*Mozzel*" in Yiddish means good luck. So—"*mozzel*," Caroline.

Samuel Gershon Balaban

A clock outside struck the quarter-hour. He pushed both envelopes back in the safe and relocked it. He waited a second behind the door in the outer room and set the burglar alarm. The corridor was quiet. He closed the office and made his way to the lavatory. There he stood on the seat and lifted the cover of the water-cistern. He dropped the three keys out of sight and replaced the cover. His mind was still juggling with the import of what he'd read. No

lawyer had drafted Balaban's will but common sense assured him it would stand up legally. He told himself he
must put the will out of his mind. It could be changed—in
any case two people's lives had to run before Caroline
Woodall would benefit. Craig wasn't a fortune-hunter.
Better the existence of the will was forgotten. He told
himself it was for Craig's sake—and the girl's. Deep
down, he knew it was himself he was protecting. Craig was
part of his future now and Caroline Woodall an interloper.
What he carried in his pockets was real. In another hour it
would be translated into known values. Cheques for the
bank—the Internal Revenue. All the bastards who'd been
drooling down his neck for the past two years.

He walked out to the stand-up snack bar on the corner,
buying a newspaper on the way. There was no one in the
tiny room but a teenager in a jacket that had been white
a week before. Glass trays were decked with pallid cold-
cuts, pies that appeared to be moulded in plastic. A few
chilled pop-bottles completed the décor.

The boy slapped a wet rag along the counter. " Tea,
mate, or coffee?"

Scott carried his cup to a stall at the window. From
habit, he opened the newspaper at the racing page. He
sipped the hot brew without knowing what he was drinking.

The teenager leaned across the counter, jerking a thumb
at the radio behind him.

"Racing's more than likely off, mate," he said conversa-
tionally. " They give it out on the news half hour ago.
Inspecting the course at ten. Bleeding weather." He worried his nose with an inquisitive finger.

Scott folded the newspaper. Outside, the snowfall came
in white flurries—no thicker than it had been before but
beginning to settle on the untrodden parts of the sidewalk.
The drive across country from Ascot would be troublesome
though the sales would hardly be affected. The idea of
bidding for a good likely chaser excited him. Somehow, fifteen thousand pounds worth of Swiss francs had to be de-

posited to his account without raising suspicion. Up to now, Craig had supplied all the answers. He wasn't likely to have forgotten this one.

The teenager was obviously caught with the desire to communicate.

" Not English, are yer?"

Scott was instantly alert. He'd spoken three words in this crummy dump yet he was leaving a memory of something out of the ordinary. He put a coin on the counter, faking a broad Scots accent.

The youth rang the coin sceptically then put it in the cash register. His sharp face was secret.

" Got an ear for it, I 'ave. You meet all sorts at this caper."

Scott left the bar and walked west. At the beginning of New Oxford Street, he hailed a cruising cab.

" Prince's Gate. Take the bridge over the Serpentine."

The north side of the park was filling with cars. The grass was already hidden, the harsh outlines of the bare trees softened by a white coating. Nearing the bridge, Scott looked through the window. A Citroën was stationary by the edge of the water. He tapped on the glass.

" Let me off here. I'll walk the rest of the way."

He waited while the driver fumbled through two thicknesses of clothing to make change. The man's mouth was wry.

" On a day like this! The best of British luck to you."

Scott made his way towards the parked car. The front door opened when he was ten yards away. He climbed in beside Van der Pouk. A man in his thirties sat in the back seat. A patch covered his right eye. The flesh on that side of his face was puckered with burn tissue. He made no sign of acknowledgment. Scott looked away quickly.

Van der Pouk was soberly elegant. His heavy jaw-line shone from the razor and he smelled of toilet water. His hat partially covered the dispatch case beside him. His inspection of Scott was brief but thorough.

"*Bon,*" he said shortly and waited for Scott to make the next move.

Scott reached inside his pocket. He spread the contents of the suède squares on the seat. Van der Pouk fitted a jeweller's loup into an eye. He bent over each item, examining it minutely. He opened his jaw like a man yawning, caught the loup as it fell and sat up straight. In that second, Scott's heart dwindled. He asked himself if the jewellery was fake. Whether Balaban had still outwitted them.

"What's wrong?" he said quickly.

Van der Pouk tapped his teeth with a fingernail. "This is all?"

Scott's feeling was of complete isolation. As if Craig and he had been cut off from the rest of the world—and the Belgian left on the far side of the fence. He produced the two blue-wrapped packages. He made no effort to be courteous.

"These don't figure in the contract."

Van der Pouk's thick forefinger riffled through the loose baguettes, chestnut eyes swimming in calculation. He made a cradle of his hands, illustrating his meaning.

"Thirty-one thousand—for everything."

Scott took a long, deep breath. "It's a deal."

The Belgian moved swiftly. He lifted his hat and swept the jewellery into the dispatch case. Twisting the upper part of his body, he addressed the man in the back seat.

"*Donne le fric.*"

His companion lifted a brown-paper package from the floor at his feet—passed it to Van der Pouk.

The Belgian's nail ripped through the covering. The Swiss francs were in four bundles, banded with bank wrappers. He broke the seal on one sheaf, peeled off twenty-eight bills and put them in his wallet. The rest of the money he pushed along the seat.

"There are a hundred thousand-franc notes in each. Do you wish to count them?"

Scott touched the top of the nearest pile tentatively. The

paper was slightly greasy to his fingers—the engraving and colouring impressive. He shook his head.

" If it's short, you'll be hearing from Craig."

Van der Pouk smiled for the first time. " I seldom make mistakes with money, my friend. Tell Craig to be careful." He peered through the windshield. A hundred yards away, a wrapped eccentric sat on a bench facing the lake. He was scattering bread to the waterfowl. Van der Pouk's hand-wave dismissed the scene. " I expect you are in a hurry."

Scott glanced over his shoulder uncertainly. Van der Pouk's companion had both hands deep in his overcoat pocket. Scott sensed that both would be glad to see the back of him.

" Give me a lift as far as Bayswater Road," he said obstinately. " I'll find a cab there."

Van der Pouk touched the starter. They drove from the park without speaking. Scott jumped out at the lights and walked west without looking back. He'd need silver for the phone call. He changed a pound in a cigar store and hurried to the nearest booth. He dialled the first of the three numbers Usher had scribbled down. There was a brief silence, a clicking of closing circuits then Craig's cautious response.

Scott spoke very close to the mouthpiece. " It's in the bag. The money's in my pocket. No hitch—no trouble."

Usher's voice was slow and distinct. " Listen to me carefully, Jamie. I'll be outside Epsom Station at eleven o'clock. I won't be able to park. You've got to be there waiting for me. As soon as you see me coming, walk on down the street. I'll pick you up."

The inside of Scott's mouth dried of saliva. He forced the words past a barrier of fear.

" What happened—why the change of plan?"

The answering whisper was barely distinct.

" Don't panic—just get here as fast as you can—Balaban's dead."

# CRAIG USHER

TUESDAY

He replaced the phone. The floor of the booth was littered with cigarette butts that he'd burned, waiting for Scott's call. He bent down, rubbed them to a handful of tobacco shreds. These he scattered outside. Everything was hushed under the persistent snowfall. The bleak grandstand and deserted concourse like disused film-sets. Only the faintest outline remained of the footsteps he'd made twenty minutes before. Visibility was down to a hundred yards. He kept close to the wall, running with head down. There was an hour to go before Jamie could be at the station. An hour until they could get out of the neighbourhood. Instinct prompted him to hole-up somewhere—to take his cargo back into the swirling flakes fast obliterating the gallops, the bushes beyond. Presentiment told him to keep moving. A police patrol was less likely than the appearance of some chance pedestrian, intrigued by a couple of vehicles seemingly abandoned.

He fastened the gate leading to the enclosure and hoisted himself through the door of the trailer. The girl hadn't changed position since Jamie had laid her on the floor. She was stretched out on her side, her face hidden under a cascade of hair. The blanket covering her rose and fell steadily with her breathing. He stepped away quietly, round the other side of the partition. He squatted by Balaban's body.

What had happened up in that remote lane seemed an age ago. He'd stopped, making a routine check on the pair in the trailer. Caroline lay as she did now. Something about the jeweller's posture had sent him into startled action. He ripped off the gag and blindfold—cut the tape

binding Balaban's wrists and ankles. Freed of restraint,
the jeweller's jaw dropped. Tortured lungs expressed one
last rush of air. A dribble of spittle ran down the side of the
slack mouth. The liver-spotted hands were still warm but
offered no resistance. Usher rolled the body on its stomach
—kneaded the flaccid shoulder muscles in a frantic attempt
to restore the jeweller's breathing. The effort was useless.
A laboured heart, over-stimulated by emotion, had ceased
to beat. It was as simple as that.

Usher looked down. The rolled eyes staring up at him
were unseeing yet he felt strangely vulnerable. As though
he needed the disguise stuffed under the seat of the Land-
Rover to save him from recognition. He spread the blanket
over the body. He emptied the hay-net, scattering dried
grass over the bundle on the floor—camouflaging the corpse
as best he could. A thousand ancestors whispered the secret
of self-preservation. His brain composed event and sequel
mechanically—almost without volition.

Jamie was thorough. He'd have done his job properly.
Balaban's office would show no sign of entry. The doors
and safe would be locked, the burglar alarm turned on. No
one in the Wessel Building could have cause for suspicion.
Balaban never went home for lunch. It would be night
before his wife became anxious. Once she turned in the
alarm, the police would locate the parked Jaguar. That's
where the search for the missing jeweller would start. It
was a matter of time before the police checked on Caroline.
Then the search would extend to Queen's Gate and her
house.

He tried to reason like a Divisional Detective Inspector
dragged from his dinner at the insistence of a frightened
woman. The investigation was uncomplicated. As yet there
was no suggestion of robbery. An elderly jeweller leaves
with his secretary to watch his horse gallop. A trainer sees
their car arrive at Epsom. He sees it leave. Later, it's found
in Hatton Garden, a block away from Balaban's office.
Some time that evening, the jeweller's wife calls Scotland

Yard, concerned about her husband's absence. Ne'ther Balaban nor Caroline can be found. Cops had few illusions. The implication was classic. It wouldn't be the first time an elderly man took off with a good-looking girl. The D.D.I. would order a routine check of hotels, the air and seaports. He'd go back to his spoiled dinner, philosophical about matters beyond his province. Only later would they get around to opening the safe.

He shut the door of the trailer behind him and climbed back into the Land-Rover. They were out of danger just as long as Jamie kept his head. First and foremost, they had to get their cargo back to the farmhouse. Not till Balaban's body was deep under Jamie's land could they risk turning Caroline loose. Time enough to decide then what to do with her. As long as she saw neither of their faces—didn't hear their voices—the worst she could tell the police was that she'd been abducted. Some smart cop would smell robbery, but his nose wouldn't be long enough to scent death.

He leaned his forehead on the edge of the steering wheel. Ever since it had happened, he'd kept the word out of his consciousnss. It was natural death—not murder. Yet a hollow voice from a courtroom persisted.

*. . . that you did, in the commission of a felony, use violence resulting in the death of Samuel Balaban.*

His lips never moved but his mind said " no " in a loud voice. He shook himself into action and set the car in motion. The four-wheel drive took its load steadily, hauling the vehicle over snow-covered turf on to the hardtop road. The risk he was running was calculated. The likelihood that he'd be stopped, that a cop would demand to look in the horsebox, was remote. He steered with one hand, groping under the driving seat for the automatic. He found it—thumbed down the safety-catch and pushed the weapon inside his jacket.

He drove for what seemed an eternity, crossing and recrossing the maze of lanes on the high ground. He avoided gas stations and bus shelters—anywhere that his perambulations might be observed and remembered. He leaned forward, peering through the sweep of the windshield wipers. Certainty strove with conjecture in his mind. Caroline, Jamie and Balaban. Each, in his own way, was a threat. One was dead—time would give him wisdom how he must deal with the other two.

It was five to eleven as he rounded the corner before the railroad station. A group of children were firing snowballs at one another, dangerously close to the edge of the sidewalk. He cut his speed to a crawl, scanning the space in front of the station exit. Suddenly he saw Scott, sheltering under a hoarding twenty yards away. He touched the horn once. Scott crossed the street at an angle that took him ahead of the Land-Rover. He ran a few steps alongside then swung himself into the cab. Snow had melted on his overcoat, saturated the brim of his hat. The scar by the side of his mouth was white against his wind-tanned skin.

"I've been here a quarter of an hour." He said it as though the time were important. He watched the speedometer needle creep up under the pressure of Usher's toe. His voice and manner were strained.

"For Christ's sake, what happened, Craig?"

Usher was concentrating on the road ahead. The County trucks were already out, men shovelling salt and sand on the slush that showed signs of freezing.

"He's dead," he answered shortly. "A heart-attack. I'll drive. You show me the way."

Scott's movements were particularly deliberate. He kicked the clotted filth from his shoes and tossed his hat behind the seat. He looked Usher full in the face.

"Show you the way *where*?"

A hundred yards in front of them, a caped policeman was slowing the traffic at the road-junction. Usher dropped down through the gears, driving with utmost care. Jamie was scared—he had to be reassured. It wouldn't be easy.

Usher spoke as casually as he could. "We're going back to Chestnut Gate. You did fine. Now get a hold on yourself."

The line of cars in front had started to move forwards again. There was no right turn. The choice was either left or straight ahead. In a few seconds he had to make up his mind. He let in his clutch. The cop was stamping his feet. He sped each passing car with a peremptory wave of the hand—as if one less solved his immediate problems. The crawling Land-Rover was only feet away. He beckoned it on impatiently.

Usher swallowed hard. "Which way, Jamie?"

Scott was sitting very straight. Not till the very last moment did he decide to answer.

"Straight ahead."

Usher touched the accelerator. The cop stepped back, avoiding the spraying muck. As the Land-Rover passed, he glanced into the cab, nodding with the friendliness of a country policeman.

Once out of town, Usher worked his way across undulating terrain in the first grip of winter. The road climbed between tight fat hedges. Left and right, the fields were scored with tractor-trails—churned where beef cattle converged on the strewn fodder. Scott had wedged himself into the far corner of the bench. Other than to give the occasional direction, he kept his mouth shut tight. His eyes were never still. For some time the sky had been lightening. The snowfall grew sparser till at last it stopped altogether. They mounted the long dragging slope, ploughing into an unbroken expanse of glittering crystals. They were five hundred feet up. Wire replaced hedges. A flock of sheep browsed on the perimeter of a copse bordering a stream. Usher swung the trailer to one side and killed his motor.

"We'd better talk, Jamie," he said quietly.

Scott's face was tight. He started emptying his pockets, stacking the bundles of money on the seat beside him. Usher caught his wrist.

"What the hell are you doing?"

Scott shrugged himself free. "Delivering. Isn't that what you want—to count your money?"

"*Our* money," replied Usher. The showdown might as well be here as anywhere. "You're in this with me, Jamie." He wrapped the cash in a paper sack and stuffed it behind the seat. Then he lit a cigarette and waited.

Scott bent over clasped hands. "I've done everything you asked, Craig. But not murder. This is the end of the line."

Everything outside was peaceful. Water washed the stone bed of the stream. The trees were wrapped in cotton. The sheep nibbled at their base. The scene had the *gmütlichkeit* of a German Christmas card. Usher slid his window down, watching the grey smoke from his cigarette hang in the still air.

"Murder's a word I don't like," he said soberly. "You'd better readjust your thinking. You've got to get it into your head that Balaban's just stopped living." He snapped thumb against forefinger. "The heart muscle went like that. If he hadn't died back there it could have been on the street—in his office. We're not to blame."

Scott turned his hands over. His fingers were locked together, white with the intensity of his grip.

"We're hauling a dead body, aren't we?" he asked flatly. "What are we going to do with it?"

Usher's cigarette made a hole in the snow-capped verge.

"What do *you* figure we should do—cart this pair to the nearest police-station and tell them we're sorry? For God's sake, Jamie. You've just emptied the man's safe. By now Van der Pouk's in Antwerp or Paris—a thousand miles away. There's no going back even if we wanted to."

Scott made a quick movement, slamming clenched fists against the dash. His eyes enforced the truth of his words.

"I can't do it, Craig. I'm scared—scared shitless."

They were long past the point of pretence. What counted now was the ability to deal with fear—to substitute certainty for the unknown. Usher spoke reasonably.

"I know it—so am I. But they're not getting us, Jamie. I want you to listen to me carefully. As long as Balaban's body isn't found, he's presumed missing. Think of nothing but this." He recapitulated his reasoning, strengthening his own assurance in the telling. He finished on the same recurring theme.

"It isn't you, or me, any longer. It's us. I never killed a man since the army stuck a gun in my hand. I don't even want to. But nobody better push me—we've got too much going for us. There's one way out—to bury Balaban so deep they'll never find him."

Scott shook his head. "A clean sheet. The bank paid off—you in a pair of Huntsman breeches and a straw in your mouth. And what have we got? A body. Isn't that something!"

Usher kept his temper. "We've got thirty-one thousand pounds behind this seat. And I'm going to make sure we get to spend it. We can go a long way with that sort of money, Jamie. You'll have to decide whether we go together or separately. No strings but no comeback. Have you got that straight?"

The sheep had left the copse. Led by an inquisitive wether they trotted towards the vehicles. The leader lifted its head uncertainly, the bell round its neck tinkling softly. The flock scampered as Scott moved his hand.

"No strings—no comeback. You're talking like some cheap hoodlum, Craig. Have you forgotten the girl—what happens to her?"

Usher made a caricature of indifference. The question was unanswerable. "We'll turn her loose when we're good and ready. To-morrow—the next day. We need time to plan. That's all, Jamie. Time. My passport's back in my room. The moment I get my hands on it, what's to stop us taking the next plane out? Anywhere you like. Brazil—for all I care, Canada."

Scott shut the window, his eyes fathomless. " A dog," he said tersely.

Usher lowered his head, arms encircling the steering wheel. He looked up, his mouth ridiculing the other's sentimentality.

" There's a good chance we spend the rest of our lives in jail unless we play this very close to the chest. And you're bellyaching about a dog."

Scott seemed to take his decision. " I guess I'm hooked, Craig. I always was hooked. I'll take my chance. Whatever you say, we'll do. But I'm staying on at Chestnut Gate."

Usher recognised the tone. This was what Jamie's father had called his cousin's " Black-Presbyterian obstinacy." Nothing short of an Act of God would alter it.

" We'll talk later," he promised. " All I'm asking is whether you're with me or against me."

Scott looked at the outstretched hand a long time before taking it.

" I ought to be asking if you're with *me*. Somebody'd better be." He hesitated, jerking his head at the trailer. " It's nearly three hours. I put that tape on real tight and it's cold. She won't know if she's got hands or feet."

Usher unlatched the door and walked back. The interior of the horsebox was dark. He could find no switch. He held a lighted match high in the air, locating the girl's still body. He knelt down beside her. Her shoulders were soft and warm under the blanket. He eased the tape strapping her wrists and ankles. He felt her flinch as his fingers touched her face. The blindfold had not budged but the pad over her mouth was saturated with moisture. He groped in his pocket for more cotton, peeling the adhesive strips from her cheek. As he took out the gag, her teeth barely missed the heel of his hand. He silenced her cry with the fresh ball of soft material, fastened it firmly in place.

*Where the willows hung, just a dream ago*—the same arms and mouth had been pleading yet responsive that warm spring day in her bedroom. For her it had been the first time. For them both, a mutual desire stronger than any thought of consequence. When it was done, they had lain close on the bed. Silent, yet sharing one another's thoughts. The month had passed normally for her. Never once had she shown any sign of regret. Somewhere she had found an understanding doctor who had provided assurance of no future pregnancy. It had been nearly two months later that she'd taken on the job with Balaban. If ever she knew the truth, he'd be as dead for her as the body on the other side of the partition. She'd remember a liar and thief—a louse who had used her to rob her employer. That it was only half-true meant nothing. Once she was free, the risk involved in seeing her again was too great to run.

He shut the trailer door and took his place at the wheel. Scott appeared from behind a tree and clambered in beside him.

" Is she all right?"

The trailer skidded off the verge, the Land-Rover grinding into the white expanse ahead.

" As right as she'll ever be," Usher said stonily. In that moment, he bade goodbye to something that mattered less to him than freedom and fifteen thousand pounds.

The hardpacked snow on the A3 moved the drivers of the oncoming traffic to unusual consideration. Cars and trucks were taken along slowly, the distance between vehicles maintained. Blue and mustard uniformed patrolmen puttered by, counselling caution at ice-locked bends. Here and there, cars had careered into the ditch, their owners walking away, leaving their wrecks pitched at strange angles. The Land-Rover was already in the outskirts of Basingstoke when Usher felt the drag on the steering column. He drove on for fifty yards, listening to the tell-tale bump from behind. He pushed his head out of the window. A boy, red-nosed with cold, was clearing the sidewalk in front of a grocery store. He leaned on his shovel, pointing at the rear of the trailer. Usher jumped out. The near back wheel was down on the rim. He felt the sweat spring in his palms and on his neck. He walked round to Scott's side of the cab, keeping his voice under control.

"We've got a flat. Where's the spare?"

Scott's gesture of alarm was involuntary. "In the trailer —hanging in the groom's compartment."

Small houses lined one side of the long street. Mean two-storeyed dwellings identical in size, shape and colour. The curtains moved in the one opposite. Behind them, the woman's face was inquisitive. Usher looked past the rash of neighbourhood stores along the street. A couple of hundred yards away, a large red sign advertised a brand of gasoline.

"We've got to get off the highway," he decided. "I'll pull in behind the garage."

He eased in the clutch, limping towards the concrete runway in front of the gas-station. He stopped twenty feet from the pumps. A man in overalls opened the office door. He stood, watching them, wiping his hands on a rag. Usher headed across, disguising his accent as best he could.

"All right if I change a wheel?—I'm in trouble."

The man took one reluctant step from the warmth of his office.

"I wouldn't unload there, if I were you. There's ice. A horse wouldn't stand up for thirty seconds."

"We're not unloading—we're empty," said Usher. "I'll only be a couple of minutes."

The attendant grinned disbelief. "And the rest, chum. Got everything you want?"

Usher nodded. Scott already had the jack out of the Land-Rover. He rammed it under the trailer's back axle. Usher pulled himself up through the small door. There was light enough to see the spare wheel screwed against the wall. He lowered it to the ground, shut the door behind him and rolled the wheel to the air-line. It needed a couple of pounds of pressure. The attendant was out of his office again, a sweater round his shoulders. He came over to stand in the lee of a store-room, viewing the performance with the superiority of a professional.

Usher's hands slipped on the lug-wrench. He felt nothing of the skinned knuckles. He lifted off the wheel, taking the good one from Scott. He spun the nuts hurriedly and waited for Scott to lower the jack. The man against the wall was dubious.

"That's a tubeless you punctured, isn't it? We don't have the gear here to repair it. Better let me fit you an inner. I wouldn't risk being without a spare in this weather."

Usher bent over the wheel. A stifled moaning was coming from inside the trailer—as if the girl sensed that help was near. Scott's face had gone grey beneath the tan. He slipped along the blind side of the vehicle and started the motor. Usher stood on the wrench to get extra pressure. To his ears the moaning came ever louder. He carried the deflated wheel back to the air-line. With this type of tyre flats usually sealed themselves for an hour or so. This one seemed to be holding pressure. It would have to do. The attendant tried again.

"I said you'd better let me put an inner tube in that spare."

Usher pushed some coins into the man's hand, his voice suddenly loud.

"I'm only going the other side of town. Thanks just the same."

Back in the cab, he lit a cigarette with a shaking hand. He sat for a while, watching the attendant through the office windows. The man donned spectacles and settled down in front of the stove with a newspaper.

"The bitch," Usher said with sudden feeling. The change of emotion was now complete. Caroline had become an enemy whose sole purpose was to put him back in a cell where he'd rot.

The blood was returning to Scott's cheeks. He shook his head like a man still numbed by the unexpected.

"He couldn't have heard anything. For Christ's sake let's get out of here, Craig."

"The bitch," Usher said again with hostility. Mouth hard, he put the convoy in motion.

They stopped once more, each in his turn gulping hot tea and hamburgers at a roadside café. The other guarded the vehicles, parked at a circumspect distance. Daylight was almost done when they rounded the last bend before the village. Usher climbed over the seat into the back of the Land-Rover. Scott took the wheel. Mrs. Parrish's cottage was already illuminated. The rest of the hamlet ensconced behind drawn curtains. Sound of the school-teacher at organ practice drifted from the church and over the vicarage wall.

The light was on in the stableyard. Someone had swept the gravel inside the concrete walk free of snow. A trampled straw-ring showed where Parrish had exercised the horses. Scott manœuvred the vehicles underneath the barn. He touched the horn and jumped down. Usher was sitting on the floor at the back of the Land-Rover. He had a clear view across the yard to the door of the tack room. Seeing Scott, the wolfhound uncoiled from a mat, stretched and went into its lumbering hop. Parrish stood in the doorway, his long cheerless face yellow under the lamp.

Scott's greeting was too low for Usher to distinguish but Parrish's answer had the penetrating pitch of the stone deaf.

"Sales? You didn't buy anything, I'll warrant." He followed Scott into the tack room, his persistent bawl echoing in the yard.

"The chestnut's leg's up agin. I been stooping it all afternoon. Mark my words, mister. That there galloping done him no good." His manner conveyed the inevitability of the disaster that followed Sabbath-breaking.

They came out again and the light went on in the chestnut's box. The heads of both men showed over the half-door. Usher went completely flat as the wolfhound loped under the barn and began sniffing the wheels of the trailer. He was able to hear the mumble and shout of the conversation. If the place were full of cops, he thought savagely, Jamie would still be feeling horses' legs. It was half an hour before Parrish left, on foot, and picking his way with a flashlamp. A few minutes more and the gate banged shut at the bottom of the driveway. Usher crawled upright, brushing the dirt from his clothes. Scott was standing in the yard, whistling softly. Usher jumped down, carrying the package of money. He avoided the dog's ponderous welcome, wiping oozing knuckles that were beginning to stiffen. He made no attempt to hide his annoyance.

" That old goat and his blethering. I thought you'd never get rid of him."

Scott was kicking straw under the bottom of the chestnut's door. He answered when he had sealed it against the draught.

" Some things have to be done my way, Craig. He'll be back at eight for stables. You needn't worry—he won't come near the house."

Too often, Usher was sensing the need for compromise —the constant subjection to Scott's sensitivity. He started towards the kitchen door.

" What we want is a large drink apiece."

Upstairs in the bathroom, he ran cold water over his hand. He tipped a bottle of iodine on the abrasions. When the sting had died, he patched his knuckles with adhesive plaster and went down. A good fire brightened the shabby sitting-room. He took the tumbler from Scott, splashed soda into two fingers of Scotch. His smile was humourless.

" The pick-and-shovel brigade. It's going to freeze hard to-night. We'll have to dig before it gets too late."

The frown lines deepened in Scott's forehead. He avoided looking directly at his cousin.

" You're not going to leave the girl out there all night?"

Usher set his glass down deliberately. " You're worrying

119

about all the wrong things, Jamie. The dog—that old plough-jockey—now it's her again. Suppose *you* tell me where we can put her. You're still serious about staying on here?"

Scott looked up. His thin face was set, eyes the colour of washed jeans challenging.

" I'm staying."

Usher shrugged. He took up his pacing, indifferent to the other's fastidiousness. However things worked out, he had to have his passport. Permanent tenants at his rooming house were a rarity. His departure wasn't likely to disturb the crone in the basement. But somehow he ought to plug the leaks in his alibi. He came to a halt in front of the fireplace.

" I've got to go to London to-morrow. If you're staying here, I'll have to arrange your share of the loot to be paid into your bank. *You'll* have her on your hands. Maybe for a couple of days. Obviously she can't stay rolled in a blanket. Is there anywhere safe in the house we can put her?"

Scott nodded. " The boxroom. You've seen it—the door next to the linen closet. There's a bed—an electric fire and a skylight. She couldn't reach it even if she stood the bed on end."

Usher ran upstairs. The boxroom door had a stout lock. There was no window other than the skylight set in the roof. A thick coating of snow covered the glass. It would keep her out of trouble till he got back from town. Too bad if Jamie had to play jailer. He could blame his own crazy obstinacy in wanting to stay on. If it hadn't been for him they could have got rid of Caroline that night. Dumped her a hundred miles away, just as soon as Balaban was underground. Now it would have to wait till his own arrangements were made. The cash converted—a seat booked on a plane. He would be sure he was three countries away before she was released. Another forty-eight hours wouldn't matter—not even if the law discovered the empty safe. It would still be Balaban they'd be looking for. Balaban and Caroline.

He went down to the sitting-room. Scott was in an arm-chair, his glass emptied and refilled.

" It'll do," said Usher. " You'll have to run me to the station in the morning. I'll send you a wire where to collect me. That'll mean Parrish is left here alone while you're gone."

Scott's voice sounded tired. " Let me worry about Parrish. It won't be the first time I've locked the kitchen door. If it comes to that, I can send him into town on the bus. There's some gear to go to the saddler's. She can yell her head off. There'll be no one to hear her."

Usher thought for a moment. He tipped the bottle of Scotch again, grateful for its comfort. " I've got a better idea—leave her so that she *can't* yell. Once we take off the blindfold you realise that I can't go near her. You'll have to put something over your face again. And don't give her a chance. She's fast and tough as a terrier. She'll be looking for the slightest mistake."

Scott stood. " We've still got to feed her."

Usher's gesture made a nonsense of the rest of the speech. He sat himself at the table, unzipped the portable machine and banged out a page of typescript. He shoved it over for Scott to read.

" I've put it all there. Make her read it. Three meals— the times she gets them. She uses the john morning and evening. And you go with her."

Scott put the sheet on the mantel. " God Almighty," he said simply.

Usher balled his shoulders. " I'd skip the squeamishness. It's our liberty we're playing with. What about Balaban?" Somehow it was easier to say than " the body." " We've got to put him where he'll never be found. Off your land, for preference."

Scott turned his back, looking into the fire. It was some time before he answered.

" Lallie Mellor's place, maybe. We can reach it over the back paddock. If you crossed the bridge with the dog yesterday, the gate in the fence would still be unlocked. The Mellors go to the house half a dozen times a year—nobody else. We could find somewhere in the woods."

Usher was unconvinced. " I'm thinking of you, not me —you're the hero. I'll be long gone if he's ever found." He smiled at the simplicity of the answer. " The church-yard. What's better than that? There must be dozens of headstones in there that nobody's looked at in years. I want to bet even the names are forgotten. It's perfect. We can go over the wall at the bottom of the lane."

Scott's objection was quick and absolute. " Fifty yards from the vicarage windows? You don't understand these people. This guy's capable of being on his knees in the church at midnight. At *any* time."

Usher relinquished the idea reluctantly. A corpse hidden in a grave seemed foolproof.

" Then it has to be the Mellors! Only not under trees. A man goes out with a dog after rabbits and you're in trouble. And it's wet there—the soil will subside. *Think,* Jamie!"

Scott asked the question bluntly. " How long before it stinks?"

Usher weighed the problem. " If we go deep enough, not at all."

The hound stretched, whining softly at Scott's knee. He touched it with quick fingers.

" There's an old carriage way along the ridge. Lallie's grandmother had it built with a kind of summer-house at the end. They had a barbecue up there a couple of years ago. The floor's made of stone-flags."

Usher swallowed the last of his drink. " Let's get it over. We'll bring her in first. The stockings and stuff are under the front seat. What you don't need we'll stick in the kitchen range."

Scott's eyes approved the decision. " I'll put blankets and sheets in the boxroom. She'll want water." He was gone five minutes. He came down, smiling a little as though expecting to share a joke. " I left the paper on her bed. That last paragraph. *This is no game. You'll take what's written here literally if you want to go on living.* What's that supposed to mean?"

Usher pulled on his gloves, wincing as the leather touched his sore hand.

" That she'd better take it literally—no more, no less."

Scott's quick move took him to the foot of the stairs. A creaking sound came from above, followed by a rattle over the tiles. Something thudded outside the sitting-room windows. He ran over and drew back the curtain. Heat had dislodged a drift from the roof. Beyond the frost-pattern on the pane, the flakes sailed down, slowly enough to time their descent. He pulled the cord.

" It's started snowing again." It was difficult to know whether he was pleased or not.

Usher buttoned his jacket. " So much the better. It'll cover our tracks."

They went out through the kitchen. The house was a mile away from the village. The steep rise intervening made observation of the stableyard impossible. Nevertheless, Usher cut the light out there. He followed the straw-ring to where Scott waited under the barn.

" As she is, in the blanket," said Usher. " You one end. I'll take the other."

He jumped up into the trailer, striking matches till he cleared the passage between the door and the prostrate girl. Scott took the weight of her shoulders. They carried her into the house, slung hammock-wise in the rough wool coverlet. They climbed the stairs, her knees sliding down against Usher's chest. He pushed away their resistant thrust impatiently. The two-bar heater had warmed the boxroom. The two men stood at the door watching her stir ineffectu-

123

ally on the bed as she felt the heat of the fire. Usher locked the door and gave the key to his cousin. Once downstairs, Scott made for the whisky bottle.

Usher flattened his hand on the cork. "When we get back, Jamie," he counselled. "It'll taste that much better."

Scott donned the stained hunting mac hanging in the kitchen, rubber boots and a cap. Usher found a yellow slicker in the hall. They unhitched the trailer and lowered the ramp at the rear. Scott's reluctance to be first up was obvious. The springs gave a little under Usher's weight. He spoke from the darkness inside.

"Can this blanket be traced to you?"

Scott's voice was uneven. "Yes."

Usher bent over. The limbs he was touching had stiffened in foetal position—knees drawn up, head pushed down towards them. He jerked the edge of the blanket. The dead load rolled off, striking against the partition. He tossed the blanket out to the yard and dragged the body down the ramp.

Scott had fetched shovels, a pick and crowbar from the tool-room. The hound jumped into the front of the Land-Rover. Usher opened the door. The animal sounded warning, deep in its throat.

Usher kept a cautious distance. "Get this bloody dog out," he ordered.

Scott came round the front of the vehicle. "He'll be all right once I'm in."

Usher grabbed his arm. "I said get him out, you goddam fool! Don't you *know* what'll happen?"

The hound went amiably with Scott. Usher heard the kitchen door close, the creak of rubber on snow as his cousin recrossed the yard. Usher lowered the tailgate. They lifted the body into the back of the Land-Rover. As the motor caught under Scott's thumb, the hound barked once. The wipers cleared V's on the clotted windshield. Scott headed into the back paddock, driving without lights. Usher had his window open, the soft wetness on his face. Visibility was down to a few yards. Scott's sense of direction appeared to be infallible. They rolled down the slope to the river. Usher recognised the humped stone bridge. Barbed wire lined the banks on the far side of the water. He opened the gate. The avenue ascended between shrouded firs, under a vaulted archway and into a coachyard. To their right were the servants' quarters of the small Georgian house. The windows were curtained. There were mats before the doors. But the house was wrapped in the tangible withdrawal of a place left without warmth or human occupation.

Scott eased the Land-Rover out of the coachyard. The road ahead clove through massed laurel and rhododendron. To the right it skirted an enormous hothouse. Something behind the glass scurried over paper. Scott's head lifted towards the sound.

" Rats." He said it dispassionately.

It was the first time either had spoken since the conflict over the dog. Usher tried to jump the gap between them.

" Is it much farther, Jamie?"

Scott chose the lane ahead. " A mile at least." The tyres were quiet on snow-packed macadam. The ground rose gently, leaving a sunken croquet lawn on their right. The banks were wild with unpruned rose bushes. They passed a deserted tennis-court, the garden roller in its centre, deep under snow. The grade grew stiffer till it flattened on the crest of the hill. Beech and poplar grew thick on the slopes each side. Stumps showed where trees had been felled to afford a clear view of the village—the galloping straight on Scott's land. The avenue ended abruptly in front of a timbered summerhouse.

" This is it," said Scott.

Usher jumped down. The summerhouse was enclosed on three sides. The fourth was left open on a terrace extending far beyond the parked car. He went inside and lit a match, shielding the flame with cupped hands. Iron garden furniture was stacked against the inner wall. The square paving stones had been laid with the care of another generation. Each was lead-keyed to its fellow, the surfaces polished by forgotten feet. He went outside, choosing a spot at the edge of the terrace. He scraped the snow away, feeling with bare fingers. The lead here had disappeared. The stones were scarred and chipped by the hooves of carriage-horses. He lowered the end of the crowbar into an interstice —leaned on it carefully. The granite square lifted. He skidded it free of its base. The stones were bedded on gravel. He prised up a second and put his gloves back on.

"Let's dig."

Scott swung the pick, loosening the gravel. They worked without let-up till Usher's thighs and back were clammy. He was standing in the hole, ground level at his chest. He pulled himself out and dropped his shovel.

"You'll have to give me a hand, Jamie."

They carried the body over and dropped it into the pit. It fell awkwardly, landing propped in a corner. Usher took the shovel and tipped the huddle of flesh and clothing over on its side. He started to spade in the earth. Behind him, Scott was retching noisily. Usher bagged the dirt displaced by the body and humped the sack over the tailgate. Scott had come back to help. It was too dark to see his face but he worked with desperate haste. They replaced the stones, rocking their joint weight so that the flags bedded down firmly. Each stone had fallen squarely in its niche. A quarter-inch gap showed around the perimeters. These Usher stuffed with the moss he had pulled out. Wet misery crept down his neck, invaded the insteps of his shoes. They stood silent, as if by mutual consent, watching the snow encroach on their handiwork. In a few minutes Balaban's grave was lost in a white expanse.

They returned to the house as they had come. Usher distributed the sack of earth on the barn floor while Scott washed the tools. He kicked straw over the ground and joined Scott in the saddle room. His cousin's face was an unhealthy colour. His manner was unashamedly relieved.

" It's the first body I've buried," he apologised.

Usher lit a cigarette. " Without a trace, Jamie. You and I. We're the only ones who'll ever know."

Scott turned on the yard light, his eyes thoughtful. He looked at his watch.

" It's gone seven. I'd better get the gag off her."

They took the bundled battledress into the warm kitchen. Usher hooked off the top of the range, dropping one suit after another on to the glowing anthracite. He added the berets and one pair of stockings. The flame soared and died.

" Never mind about feeding her now," he instructed. " She can eat when we do. She'll probably want the john. You better go up—you've got to start sometime."

Scott's face was reluctant. " You can't do it to a woman, Craig. I've taken the key out of the bathroom door. She can't barricade herself in."

Usher dropped the cover back on the range. " She's your responsibility. But watch it."

Scott settled the dog on its bed. It growled uncertainly as he pulled the nylons over his head. Usher was two steps behind him going up. He waited behind Scott's door, listening. He heard the girl move as she was untied—the sharp staccato of her heels across the landing. The bathroom door closed. Scott's feet sounded outside. The door opened again. There was a sudden scuffle in the boxroom. Minutes passed then Scott came out hurriedly. He turned the key in the lock and went downstairs. By the time Usher joined him, Scott had the nylons off. He knuckled the hair from over his ears and poured himself a large drink.

" *That* I can do without! You were right. As soon as we got back in the room she tried to let me have it in the balls."

" And?"

Scott answered from the depth of his arm-chair. " She missed. Now she's on the bed. I fixed her so that she won't give any trouble for a while."

Usher moved uneasily, remembering a summer evening

127

—the dust acrid in his nose as he stood helpless watching her fight a horse maddened by flies. It plunged viciously against the tree, doing its best to break her leg between saddle and wood. She had sat, white-faced but determined, till the animal quietened. Only then had she slipped from the saddle, neither conscious of courage nor aware of his own fear.

" Don't give her a chance," he said sombrely. " She'll keep trying."

He spread the Swiss bills on the table, counting as he made a fresh package of the money. Van der Pouk's calculations were accurate to the fraction of a dollar. He looked up.

" You can start drawing against this to-morrow. I've got a guy in London, a lawyer. For fifty quid he'll produce a set of documents that'll cover this payment to your bank. It's worth it, just in case you're ever asked to explain."

Scott's glass was empty. He applauded sarcastically. " That's what I like about you, Craig. You think of everything. What's fifty quid? I say onwards and upwards with Usher."

His cousin's stare was speculative. " This is just a suggestion—I'd take it easy with the bottle while I'm gone."

Scott's eyes were bright with challenge. He gave himself another drink without leaving his chair.

" But this is to-day, my huckleberry friend. Don't you think it calls for a celebration? I've emptied a man's safe and buried his body."

Usher tied the bundled money with string. It was better that Jamie worked it out of his system one way or another. He was conscious of the sagging weight of the automatic in his pocket. He laid the gun on the table in front of him.

" What do you think I feel, nothing?" he asked quietly.

Scott lifted himself by the arm-rests. Usher sat still as the other came over. Scott took the automatic, ejected the clip of shells then replaced them. His finger spun the weapon back across the polished table top.

"What *do* you feel, Craig? About her, for instance. You want me to believe you didn't set her up for this. But you can still dump her in a field—take off and never see her again."

Usher's thumb clicked the catch to safety-position. "I'll give it to you straight, Jamie. What I feel about her is my business."

Scott's grin grew malicious. "You'd like to think that, sure. But it could easily be everybody's business. How would this read in some scandal sheet. CROOK ABDUCTS HEIRESS BY MISTAKE—MARRIES HER AFTER FLIGHT TO AVOID ARREST."

The ring of doubt eased in Usher's mind. How could he have missed the classic way of destroying damaging testimony. Even if Caroline learned the truth later, as his wife she could never give evidence against him. And who else *was* there to give evidence? For the last few hours he had seen her as a proven enemy. The thought of marriage changed nothing. She was an enemy to be used and at the end of it all, divorced. Only first, marriage. He had no idea how long the formalities took. Maybe he could get her to leave the country with him—have the ceremony abroad. He needed time to think. Something in Scott's speech disturbed him.

"I don't know why I never thought of it," he admitted. "There's only one thing wrong with your headlines. She's no heiress."

Scott started to laugh, his mouth and chest working uncontrollably till at last he collapsed in his chair, breathless.

Usher looked at him curiously. "You'd better fill me in. What's the gag?"

Scott's eyes were remote. "There's no gag. It's life kicking you up the arse, Craig. There was a will in Balaban's safe. When the pair of them die, she inherits everything."

Usher's arms had gone completely stiff. He could hear the thudding in his own chest.

" Now why would you bother inventing a thing like that, Jamie?" he asked carefully.

Scott seemed to find the suggestion hilarious. " Why indeed! I read the will from beginning to end." He remembered the lawyer's name with difficulty but ploughed into a paraphrase of Balaban's letter to Caroline. " ' In six months not a cross word—always the smile.' She ought to be grateful to you. You've done half the work for her." He rubbed his eyes and mouth nervously.

Usher came round the table, holding the gun. He stood over Scott's chair, pressing the barrel against his cousin's chest.

" I want the truth, Jamie."

Scott looked down, his face quite suddenly rational. He pushed the gun away.

" Don't ever do that again," he said passionately. " I don't lie and I don't scare—I've known you too long."

Usher's mind fogged. He dragged himself out of the Amazon Jungle where for some reason he found himself with Jamie—aged eleven and fourteen—in search of the lost Colonel Fawcett. He dropped the gun on the table. The money she might inherit mattered to him neither one way nor another. All it meant was that she wouldn't stay lonely for long.

" I'm sorry, Jamie," he said quietly. " I don't know what got into me."

The dog barked from the kitchen. Scott peered through the window. " It's Parrish." He straightened his tie in the mirror. Shock had completely sobered him. " If I give him a hand with the chores, we'll get rid of him that much quicker."

Usher waited in front of the fire. Again and again he went over the implications of Scott's news. It was half an hour before his cousin returned, shaking the snow from his mac.

" He's taken the saddle home. He'll get the nine o'clock

bus into town. It'll be five before he's back. I told him I'd
do stables myself to-morrow night. He's satisfied."

They ate a scratch meal in the kitchen. Scott had kept a
bowl of spaghetti warm on the stove. He put it on a tray,
added a glass of milk and pulled the nylons over his head.

Usher started stacking the dishes in the sink. " Watch
her," he warned again. He heard the bathroom plug pulled
upstairs. It was five minutes before Scott came down,
carrying the untouched food. He peeled off the stocking-
mask.

" She won't eat. Just drank the milk. She's in bed. I
left her untied."

Usher balled the wet dish-cloth, aiming it at the drying
board. " Has she said anything yet?"

Scott lifted his shoulders. " No. She just looks. The
paper you typed has gone. I think she's put it in her bag."

" Then get it back in the morning," said Usher. It was
a few minutes to nine. He went into the sitting-room and
turned on the radio. As soon as the station was on beam, he
lowered the volume. They sat opposite one another, listening to the plummy voice pass from weather to parliament
without change of intonation. The announcer's next words
had both men sitting upright.

. . . Samuel Balaban, a Hatton Garden jeweller, has been
reported missing since this morning. Mr. Balaban, who
recently exhibited at the International Jewellery Fair at
Burlington House, is known to have returned from Epsom
where he had been watching one of his racehorses exercise.
His car, a grey Jaguar, licence number 875 EPB, was found
parked near his business premises. There has been no trace
of him since. Police dogs were used in an attempt to pick up
scent from the car but the search there was quickly abandoned. A spokesman for the family told our correspondent
that Mr. Balaban had been in poor health for some time.
Will anyone knowing his whereabouts or who can give
information likely to assist police inquiries please communi-

cate with New Scotland Yard. Telephone number, White-hall 1212."

Usher cut the radio, his face troubled. "They don't say a word about the girl. Why? Are you sure you left that office exactly the way you found it?"

Scott's answer was categorical. "I already told you. I did what you said. Nothing more, nothing less."

Usher worried the thought. "The police must have gone to the Wessel Building. They'll find out from people on the same floor that Caroline hasn't been seen to-day. Yet nobody mentions her. I don't like it, Jamie." He took a few paces and stopped. He started to flick his fingers loosely from the wrist.

Scott's face was dubious. "Why don't we get rid of her now? Drive north or somewhere and just dump her?"

"To-day, to-morrow," said Usher. "What difference?" A quick memory jolted him. "Get her bag," he said suddenly.

Scott grabbed the makeshift mask and ran upstairs. He came down, carrying a green suède bag. Usher tipped out the contents at his feet. A wallet, keys, make-up and some change. The paper he had typed, a neat square hidden away in a side compartment. He unzipped the other side. It was empty. Somewhere there should have been her diary —the number of his rooming house in it. He tried desperately to remember where he had last seen the small leather book. On the table by her bed—on her desk at Balaban's office. *Where?* The exact place eluded him. He spoke more for himself than for Scott.

"Ah, the hell with it. Somebody at the Yard's playing Hawkshaw."

Scott put the guard in front of the fire. "I don't budge an inch, Craig. Whatever you decide, I'm staying put. No one's ever seen me. You'll be out of the country. And Balaban'll be missing permanently. What *can* the police do?"

Usher slid his feet out of his shoes, warming his toes.

The moment Caroline was back in circulation, she'd be answering a lot of questions herself. The law would put a tail on her, tap her phone. To get near her with a proposal of marriage, he'd have to duck half the Yard. It all needed careful thought. The sudden strength of Jamie's position was somehow ironical.

"I don't know what they can do," he said finally. "It's just a feeling that I've got. Between now and to-morrow night, I'll have to make up my mind about her. What time's the first good train?"

"There's an express at seven-eleven. Two stops to Waterloo."

"That'll do me," said Usher. "Now let's get some sleep."

# JAMES SCOTT AND CRAIG USHER

He waited where he had dropped Usher, a hundred yards from the station entrance. The hound sat large beside him, tawny-eyed as an eagle. Its ears pricked at the train beyond the railings. Scott saw Usher's silhouette stark as he made his way along the corridor. He reversed the Land-Rover. All night it had snowed without interruption. The weather forecast promised more of the same. The seven o'clock news had been grim with reports of blocked roads and blizzards to the west. The waste of Dartmoor was cut off —whole communities in Cornwall—helicopters already dropping supplies to isolated radar installations.

He started homeward under a grey sky that hung low. Once out of town he was back in a world of silence. The road, the hedges that bordered it, were a painful white glitter in his headlamps. There was little traffic—a few buses and trucks—the old tractor following a single yellow eye, its pilot muffled like a man from Mars. Scott drove slowly, the four-wheel drive churning through the banked drifts. The siren at the sawmill was blowing eight o'clock as he turned into the stirring village. He braked outside the butcher's, on impulse.

Scanlon was in thigh boots, hosing the scummed saw-dust through the back door. The butcher's hands and face were as red as the chilled carcasses hanging against the tiled walls. It was months ago that Scott had caught him, fur-tively popping a piece of raw meat into his mouth. Ever since, Scott avoided looking the man in the face.

He crossed the slippery floor carefully, pulling out his cheque-book.

"Have you got any idea how much I owe you?—I don't have the bills with me."

Scanlon went into the small office. He riffed through a clip of papers. "That's since August, look. You mean the lot, Mr. Scott?"

"The lot." Scott wrote his cheque. "You can give Parrish the receipt when he comes for dogmeat."

The butcher rang his cash register, his face sly with curiosity. "Major Mellor was in—asking if I knew the gentleman you got staying with you."

Scott was cautiously indifferent. "There's nobody staying with me. Why would he ask you, anyway?"

Scanlon's manner grew confidential. "I mean the gentleman who was here a couple of days ago. It's all over the village, what happened, Mr. Scott. I say serve him right. And that's what I told Fred Allen." He dropped the local cop's name with unction.

Scott glanced across the street at the silent pub. If Mellor had filed a complaint, it was a matter of time before the constable would be up sniffing round the house.

"What's Allen got to do with it?"

Scanlon shook his head. "Nothing. Not officially, like. We were talking, that's all. The major's a bad man to cross, sir. 'E's still living in the past. *Mrs.* Mellor, now . . ."

Scott took the innuendo. From vicarage to sawmill, these people stripped him naked behind closed doors—a foreigner suspect of credit and morals. He answered with calculated threat.

"I'll tell you something for your own good, Scanlon. You've been short-weighing me for six months. There's something else—you can pass it on to Allen. Chief constables don't take kindly to cops who gossip. Do I make myself clear?"

The butcher's face was shocked. "That's libel as I see it, Mr. Scott."

"Scandal," corrected Scott. "And not even that. We're on our own here. Anyway you wouldn't want me to have to prove what I said."

He dropped off another cheque at the combined grocery-

store and gas-station. The church was lighted as he drove
by. He pictured the few huddled in unheated aisles, seeing
their faith, hope or charity no different to that of the
butcher or Mellor. Non-conformity offended them as
sharply as the smell of fear a dog.

The house was as he had left it, Parrish's straw-ring
hidden under a fresh coating of snow. There was no question of exercising horses while this lasted. He made a mental
note to cut down on oats. Craig would be back to-night—
and, with luck, gone to-morrow. Strange how yesterday the
idea of sharing the place had been good to think about.
Now all he wanted was Craig out of it.

He kicked off his rubber boots in the kitchen. He climbed
the stairs in his slipsocks and put an ear against the boxroom door. There was no sound from inside. It was eight-
thirty and gone. But dragged from the light of day—
trussed, gagged and blindfolded—she could still go on
sleeping. He caught himself quickly. What the hell—*he'd*
slept hadn't he? He tiptoed downstairs and brewed tea.
For some reason, he found himself searching the refrigerator
for food that would tempt her to eat. . . . He pulled the
stocking over his head with a sense of embarrassment—
like a man who has run a practical joke into the ground.
He unlocked the door. The boxroom smelled of sleep and
her scent. She was sitting up in bed, her forehead touched
by the light of the fire that had burned all night. Her
clothes hung neatly on the chair. He saw the firm round-
ness of a breast before she had time to cover it with the
sheet. He walked across to the bed and put the tray on the
floor, ready for the first sign of revolt.

She watched his every movement, her eyes intent on his
hands.

"You're not Craig. Who *are* you? Why are you keeping me here?"

Shock bludgeoned him back through the years—to a time
in the playroom of the Don Valley house. The summer
smell of wall-flowers heavy through the open window. His

father on the flagged walk outside, stern with the promise
of punishment.

"*Put away your toys, Jamie, and go to the library. I
want to talk to you.*"

Somehow he managed to get outside and close the door.
He walked haphazardly across the sitting-room, looking
down at the phone. But he had no idea where he might
reach his cousin. "*You're not Craig,*" she'd said. The
implication was clear. He sat heavily in the chair, labori-
ously retracing every mile of the drive from Epsom. Suddenly he knew. The garage where they'd stopped to
change the wheel—Craig paying off the attendant. His
cousin's voice boomed in Scott's memory. He lit a cigarette,
defeated. This was the fear that he'd carried concealed
from the beginning. Last night they'd sat in this room,
fatuous with schemes about marriage. While upstairs on
the bed was the one person who knew enough to destroy
them both. The probabilities piled in his head. For all he
knew, there was a record of his relationship with Craig at
Canada House. The thought sent his hand to his mouth.
He was far too near the edge. His cousin out of the
country, he would have stayed on here comfortably waiting
for the police to assemble their jigsaw.

He went out to the kitchen, doing the chores mechanically as he tried to fashion safety out of disaster. This much
was sure—it was impossible for Caroline to know that
Balaban hadn't been driven back to Hatton Garden. As
far as she was concerned, it was still only robbery. He had
to talk to her again. This time, he threw the stockings on
the fire and went up as he was. He unlocked her door. She
had eaten most of the food and was dressed. She sat on
the bed, legs tucked under her. She studied his appearance
thoroughly.

"I knew you weren't Craig—but you look like him," she
said shrewdly. "The mouth and chin. What are you, a
brother?"

He leaned his back firmly against the door. "You better

137

get one thing straight. You're a long way from civilisation. Yell your head off, there's no one to hear you."

She nodded her head as though he only told her what she already guessed.

"What have you done with Mr. Balaban?" she demanded.

"He's safe enough," said Scott shortly. "Where you'll be if you behave yourself. Listen to me and use your head. Nobody means you any harm. You walked yourself right into this situation."

She was twisting the topaz on her finger. The candy floss hair slid as she lifted her head.

"Of course, you'd have the right clothes and manners and you wouldn't like to be called a common thief. Didn't you know Mr. Balaban's an invalid? What sort of people are you anyway, kidnapping an old man and a woman?"

He viewed her sourly. She was the kind who'd drive words into a man's head, like nails into wood.

"You're a fool," he told her. "And your mouth'll get you into trouble."

Her eyes were unfrightened. "I've got nothing to say to you anyway. But a lot to your brother or whoever he is."

Scott shrugged. "Suit yourself. But get this right. Balaban's safe is empty. Nothing you or the police can do will alter that. Your game's to get out of here as quickly as you can. A civil tongue will help."

She hacked through the sense of his speech. "A civil tongue. My *God*, what a fool I've been! At least you're Craig's confederate—do you know what he was to me?"

He made a show of understanding. "Sure I know. You slept with him. Congratulations. You and four hundred other women."

Her voice changed, deadly with the intensity of her contempt.

"I might have known he'd tell you about that. Well, you can give him this message since he's too big a coward to face me himself. I'm going to do my best to put you both in prison where you belong."

He picked up the tray, tired of her pretentiousness.

"That's a message I'll let you deliver yourself. You're just enough of a fool to do it."

He kicked the door shut behind him. The turn of the key was final but solved nothing.

: :    : :

The lawyer's chambers were high above the river, the building a brightly-lit shaft of steel and glass in the grey London morning. Warm air inside bathed two-and-a-half miles of corridor, five hundred suites of offices. Double doors and windows protected the privacy of the room where Usher sat. The deep shelves behind his back were black, red and gold with case-law and statute-book. The man across the desk laid the mouthpiece of the dictaphone beside the pile of money. His movements were precise. The freckled skin on his bald head matched that stretching from cheekbone to jaw. A polka-dotted bow-tie lessened the severity of his dark suit. He tilted a little over the neatness of his papers.

"That's everything, then, Craig. I'll have the deed of conveyance drawn up in favour of James Scott. It'll cover a payment of £15,500 to his bank. Your affair's simple. I'll cable the Marschall bank this morning and arrange immediate credit against signature and presentation of passport. Have you any idea when you'll be in Zurich?"

The airplane ticket was in Usher's pocket, the booking open. The flight he chose depended on what he decided about Caroline Woodall.

"To-morrow," he said. "The next day at the latest."

The lawyer's smile was professional and meaningless. "A bit different to the last time we met, Craig. I couldn't be happier that things seem to be working out for you. The maxim's a sound one—in for a penny, in for a pound." His eyes were suddenly sly.

139

Usher found the reference unwelcome. Rifkine's manner
had been exactly the same that day in the cells underneath
the Central Criminal Court building. He had accepted
Usher's sentence with the cheerfulness of one not obliged to
serve it. A wily operator who took a verdict of guilty as
calmly as he did his fat fee, prepaid. He'd demanded five
per cent for the transfer of funds to Switzerland. But
against that he neither answered nor asked profound questions.

Usher collected his hat. "I'll be seeing you, Nat." Both
men smiled carefully at a proposition they judged unlikely.

Rifkine swept money and papers into a drawer and
double-locked it. He opened a private door to the corridor.

"Be lucky," he said lightly and Usher was alone.

The hired car was parked at the rear of the Savoy Hotel.
The chauffeur touched his cap. Usher settled his shoulders
in the deep upholstery.

"Twenty-two, Belton Square—that's behind the Earl's
Court station."

The square was filthy with brown slush. Blown refuse
had frozen in the snow behind the railings. It was gone
eleven and the house would be empty. Usher's call from
the lawyer's office had gone unanswered.

"I'll be a quarter of an hour," he told the driver.
"You're all right for parking."

A film of ice added to the bottle-strewn hazard of the
steps. He fitted his latch-key. All he needed were his bags
and passport, he'd leave a note where the manageress would
find it. The hallway was close with the same smell of
cooking greens, the sharp wild odour of tomcat. There was
nothing for him on the message board. His foot was on the
first rung of the staircase when the door of the basement flat
was opened. The manageress peered up, squinting against
the light. She spoke briefly over her shoulder to the two
men behind her.

"That's him."

They ran easily up the stairs. The taller took up position

behind the street door while his partner stopped at the staircase. It was the shorter man who spoke.

" Mr. Usher—Craig Usher?"

Usher turned slowly, gauging the distance to the door— his chance of going through a window at the back. Instinct kept his step down to the hall easy, his voice controlled.

" I'm Craig Usher, yes. What do you want?"

" Police officers, Mr. Usher." The shorter man showed a warrant card. The manageress had crept half-way up her own stairs, cats wreathing her legs. She waited there expectantly. The detective looked ill-at-ease. He hitched a shoulder at Usher.

" Isn't there somewhere we could talk?"

Usher fought the clamour in his head, forcing himself to preserve a show of calm. The team of detectives was classical in composition. Over by the door—the hardnosed heavy, his appearance a threat of violence. The man who had spoken the friendly foil.

" Upstairs," he answered. His room would stand a frisk. The gun had been left at Chestnut Gate. Even if they discovered the tools hidden under the bath, he could deny all knowledge. If they wanted to search him, all they'd find would be an airplane ticket. He led the way up. He unlocked his room, taking in the milk bottle left outside the door. He touched a match to the broken gas-fire and straightened his back.

" Let's make it quick," he invited. " I've got things to do."

The narrow room was too small for the three of them. The younger cop leant his buttocks against the dressing table. Flannels and sports-jacket, the light tweel raglan and classless accent—all bore the stamp of the police college.

" We're making inquiries about Miss Caroline Woodall. Could you tell us when you saw her last?"

Usher lowered himself on the foot of the bed. He was sure the room hadn't been entered since he had left. There was only one way they could have a line on him. Caroline's

141

diary—it must have been found at her house. This pair was from the Yard. It would have been too simple to check him out with the Criminal Records Office. He had to play it as they would expect. An outraged rogue unjustly accused. His manner was just short of indignant.

"Caroline Woodall, eh? That's a new angle, isn't it? What are you doing—investigating my sex-life? She's over twenty-one."

The taller of the two cops perched himself on Usher's suitcases. His fingers fell naturally against the catch of the top bag. He clicked it open and shut, idly. The younger man spoke reasonably.

"Don't make our job harder than it already is, Mr. Usher. We didn't come here to embarrass you. The girl's mother thought you might be able to help. Miss Woodall's been missing since yesterday."

Usher's wave took in the confines of the room. Something about the man's bearing gave him new confidence.

"Well, she isn't here, is she?"

The man sitting on the suitcases spoke for the first time.

"Nor were you, last night."

The bed creaked under Usher's weight. "What of it? Do I have to give you people notice every time I spend a night away from home? Suppose I told you that I haven't seen Caroline Woodall since Sunday?"

The younger cop smiled pleasantly. "You'd be giving us something to go on—something to tell her mother. Where would that have been—at the mews?"

Usher leaned forward, his answer precise. "At her house, yes. I had a meal there—we talked for a while. I left around ten."

The cop was persistent. "I'm sorry to have to put it to you this way. Her mother thinks that Miss Woodall might have spent the night with you. Is that true or not?"

It was certain the police had been to the mews house. They'd probably found her diary. But they still couldn't be certain of anything. Either his police record or Caroline's mother had put him at the top of the list to be interrogated.

He answered steadily. "You asked me when I saw her last. I told you. If you want anything else, you'll get it in the presence of my lawyer."

The second cop's mouth was frankly hostile. "You're just the sort of clever bastard I *like* to take in. A night in the cells cuts people like you down to size. Where were you thinking of going, anyway?" He rapped the suitcase he was sitting on.

Usher dropped the false courtesy. "Slippery Rock, Manitoba. And you know something—all you'll retire with will be flat feet. Now get out of here and tell her mother what you like. If you come back without a warrant, I'll hit you with a suit for wrongful arrest. And don't think I can't."

The younger man broke in quickly. "Leave it, Harry. I'm sorry we had to bother you, Mr. Usher. You know the way it is. If you *should* hear from Miss Woodall, perhaps you'll let us know."

Usher was now completely sure of himself. He came to his feet. "I'll dial 999."

He waited on the landing till they were off the premises. Then he ran up to the bathroom. The tools were still in their bag, undisturbed. He left them there and opened the window. The two detectives were on the far side of the square, walking east. He went back to his room, curious and with a sense of anti-climax. They had made no attempt to search either him or his belongings. It could only mean that either the police hadn't tried to open Balaban's safe or hadn't been able. It was important to know which. The first meant that they were still only looking for two missing people. Nobody could stop him leaving the country. The marriage idea was out of the question now. He had to have time to collect his money in Zurich—to cover his tracks completely—before Caroline could be turned loose. The passport in his pocket made a reassuring bulge. He carried his bags to the hallway and yelled down to the basement.

The manageress met him belligerently, grey stockings wrinkling round her legs.

He showed his teeth at her. " White Slave Traffic. I guess you always knew it. You were next. Here's a week's rent in lieu of notice." He put the money on the top stair.

She clutched weakly at the nearest cat. " I'm going to see my solicitor . . ." she started half-heartedly. Suddenly she scurried behind her door and bolted it.

He threw his door-key on the hall table and banged the street door after him. His appraisal of the square, in the few steps from porch to car, was both concealed and rewarding. A laundry truck, parked diagonally, commanded the only exit to the Earl's Court Road. About as exciting to look at, he thought, as yesterday's teabag. Yet the motor inside the hood would mill up to a hundred miles an hour with explosive acceleration. The wheels would be fitted with disc brakes and high speed tyres. Behind that innocent-looking exterior was a crew of specialists. Drivers, radio-operator—cops trained to trail a suspect without arousing suspicion. Unless he happened to be as smart as they were. Everything about the truck was phoney except the name and address painted on the side. Check it out and you'd come up with a legitimate business. Only you'd find the proprietor was an ex-cop on the retired list.

The hired limousine rolled off. He had no need to turn his head to know that the truck had pulled out after them. Since the beginning of this new phase, police-procedure had been predictable. First the shock assault, designed to leave him free but shaken. Now he was supposed to run—to lead them to what they were looking for. What that was, he didn't yet know. With any sort of luck he'd find out in a few minutes. He paid off the driver at West London Air Terminal. He'd picked the man up at the head office, giving his own name. The law would show no profit there.

He carried his bags over to the left-luggage counter. He took his stub to a bench—read the fine print with the nervous aimlessness they'd be expecting of him. Most of the

144

people in the hall were clustered around the check-in points. He made a survey of those without baggage. Which of them was it? The Bowler Hat and Briefcase—the Scoutmaster in tweeds—the face with the sun-lamp treatment and dark glasses. It could even be the girl with the legs and the astrakhan coat. They had them all shapes these days working out of the Yard. His next move should bring one of them out into the open. He came to his feet as the flight announcement echoed through the building. The very sound of the place-names gave him a feeling of security. *Karachi—Montevideo—Istanbul.* He strolled across the hall to the bus-bays. Frozen airstrips were diverting some of the long-distance jets to Shannon and Gatwick. The European flights were still leaving from London Airport. He joined the queue for the Amsterdam bus. At the moment of boarding, he walked back into the hall. Making no attempt to conceal himself or his haste, he ran up the stairs. He shut himself in a telephone booth in front of the cafeteria.

Without knowing who he expected to answer, he dialled Caroline's number. A man came on the line—quiet and insistent. Usher replaced the receiver hurriedly. He pictured the cop in the silent house. There were probably two —they hunted in pairs. He found the jeweller's home number in the book. He fed more coins into the slot and redialled. The answering voice was anxious and fluttering.

He made his own accent undistinguishable. " Is this Mrs. Balaban? U.P. Newsroom. I'm sorry to have to disturb you at a time like this, Mrs. Balaban, but there's a rumour running round Fleet Street that your husband's insurance company is concerned by his disappearance. Naturally, we want our report to cause you as little distress as possible. Would you like to make a comment?"

The woman's whispered distress went beyond pretence. " No. There's nothing to do with insurance—just my husband. *Please* don't telephone any more." She hung up on him.

He left the booth, his face thoughtful. If the law didn't know of the robbery, why the sustained interest in him? The police didn't mount a production like this for nothing. Someone high-up at the Yard had added the phone number in Caroline's diary to Usher's record and played the result as a hunch. No matter—whoever was following him had to come into the open some time. He was over by the B.E.A. Reservation Desk when he knew he had drawn his man. The reflection was in the glass doors leading to the bus-bays. Round-faced and youngish, dressed in nondescript clothes. His perusal of his newspaper was as single-minded as a monk's of his breviary. Usher turned, took a few paces and retraced them—a man uncertain what he should do next. The newspaper barely moved but Usher noted it. That was one of them—the other wouldn't be far away. Mrs. Balaban's manner had been natural, her answer spontaneous. If the police suspected a crime, they had no proof. There would be no move to arrest him—just the surveillance. They had made one basic error. When the quarry was experienced, the hunt was difficult. He was about to give this pair a lesson that would do them no good with their superiors.

He rambled over to the Inquiry Desk and asked for paper and envelope. He leaned on the counter, aware that he was being watched. He had led them here. His actions since had been in character. Those of a man whose experience with the police made him suspicious, whether he was innocent or not. The fake boarding of the bus had proved it. Now the double-bluff was in play. They had to believe two things. That he knew he'd been followed—that he thought he'd shaken those in pursuit.

He composed the letter carefully.

Dear Caroline,

I've been trying to reach you for two days without success. I got the message very clearly when finally a man's voice answered the phone. I'm not asking who it was—nor where you've been since Sunday. When a good thing comes to an end, somebody has to make the first move. But this is no valid reason for involving the other party in unpleasantness.

The police have just been round to Belton Square asking me when I last saw you—if I knew where you were and the like. As far as I can make out, your mother has reported you missing. She had the bad judgment to suggest me as the likeliest person to help.

I said nothing except that I hadn't seen you since Sunday. With that the police left. Unfortunately for me, the management asked me to leave too. They don't take police visits lightly in Earl's Court. Obviously my new address won't be of any interest to you. I'm leaving this at your house on the assumption that it will reach you sooner or later. Two things in closing. Put a gag on your mother and keep the police out of my hair.

Craig.

He gummed the envelope. The letter would be opened long before Caroline read it. Its strength lay in the implications based on exposed facts. He retrieved his bags and carried them to the cab without a backward glance. He maintained this indifference all the way to Euston Station.

The booking-hall was crowded. He took his place in a line of ticket-buyers and paid for a single to Edinburgh. He spent a few minutes in front of the Departure Board, noting train times on a piece of paper. The immediate scene was typical. Porters shuffling behind piled baggage, harassed women with children, the customary pair of military policemen, pipe-clayed and arrogant, dwarfing their furtive prisoner. He saw no sign of the man with the newspaper. He strolled over to the cigarette stand, bought a couple of packs and matches. He angled his stance so that he saw the exit without looking directly at it. The burly individual there seemed a little too casual. He was in a heavy overcoat and tweed cap and had cop's eyes in a farmer's face. Usher

147

pocketed the handful of change, certain that this was the other member of the team.

He took up his load with difficulty, using two hands for three bags, and called another cab. He gave the driver Caroline's address and relaxed behind the strong black tobacco. A vicious east wind had been blowing for an hour, blocking fresh falls but crusting hard the snow on the ground. Hyde Park was abandoned to dogs and children, the faces of the last drained of colour by the glaring whiteness everywhere. The cab wheeled into the mews. Usher's stomach tensed with the faint beginning of nausea. This was their game he was playing, but the rules were his own invention. The cab halted in front of the girl's house. He jumped out and pushed the letter through the mail flap. A second's inspection told him that the key on the string had been removed. He walked away, feeling rather than seeing the curtains move in the room upstairs. His instruction was loud enough for the man up there to hear.

" Seventy-nine, Cromwell Crescent."

The laundry-truck made its reappearance at the junction on Queen's Gate. It cruised alongside the cab, the driver chewing mechanically. Usher turned his head. The man wore white overalls and cap. They inspected one another with the blankness of strangers caught at the lights. The signals changed. A hundred yards on, the truck was lost to sight again. Usher paid off the cab. The apartment block was old-fashioned, red-brown and sombre in Edwardian style. He hauled his luggage into the narrow hallway and looked back. The burly cop was coming along the pavement, thirty yards away. A coal-fire burnt in the hall. The porter's voice came from the depths of a leather chair fitted with a cowl.

" If it's for Mr. Cole, sir, they're away—abroad till February." Age and recognition of Usher kept him in his seat.

Usher nodded. He'd met Caroline here for the first time.

The journalist and his wife were acquaintances over the years. Their absence was no news to him.

He leant into the chair. " I wondered if Miss Woodall had been round recently—since Sunday, I mean."

The old man gave it thought. " That's the tall gel, isn't it—Mrs. Cole's friend? No—I ain't seen her in a month, sir."

Usher was already at the top of the steps leading to the basement. The stout cop had gone by once. It wouldn't be long before he showed himself inside. Usher pointed down. " I've got a train to catch. This gets me to the subway station quicker, doesn't it ?"

The porter was unenthusiastic. " Ah, but mind how you go up the outside steps, sir. I can't do nothing with 'em in this weather. It's the Chinese," he added mysteriously. " Traipsin' the muck with 'em."

Usher picked up his bags. The passage below was half-blocked by bicycles and perambulators. A short flight of stone-treads gave access to the street. He ran awkwardly past the lines of parked cars, ducked into the pub on the corner. Ground glass protected the anonymity of those inside. He watched from the end of the bar where the window was clear. A couple of minutes went by. Then the burly cop hurried out of the back entrance of the apartment building. He stood for a moment, looking up and down the street. The direction of his cautious trot took him beyond the pub and out of Usher's view.

Usher heard the woman's repeated request and faced her. He saw the room for the first time. There was a bird in a cage on the bar. Against the far wall, half a dozen tables were set for lunch. The atmosphere was warm and friendly. He picked up the menu, smiling.

" I'll take the steak-and-kidney pudding. And half a bottle of champagne."

He loitered over his food, satisfied with his performance. By now Jamie would have the telegram telling him to meet the train at Andover instead of Basingstoke. It was twenty

149

miles on but nobody at the station would know either of them. It was hard to say how the police would interpret his antics. The way he had shaken them left a loophole. It was possible that they'd think they had lost him and not vice-versa. The report they turned in would be interesting.

He paid his bill and stood at the end of the bar. The scene outside was innocuous. He picked up his bags, fluking a cab on the corner.

The train was already waiting under a head of steam. He found a window-seat in a first-class compartment, sure now that he was not being followed. The two business men opposite were launched on the Common Market. Beside him, an over-scented woman was reading a magazine, her eyes remote behind a short veil. She was fifteen years older than Caroline but they had the same fine nose and skin texture. She looked up, conscious of his scrutiny. He shifted in his seat, turning towards the window. His skinned knuckles were sore—the old hockey break in his shoulder ached with the cold. Nothing a hot sun and lazing wouldn't cure.

The guard's whistle echoed in the vaulted station, shrill above the hiss of steam. The reading lamps paled in the light of day. Beneath the viaduct, whole trains stood idle in the marshalling yards. On his right extended the panorama of the river—the plumed smoke of fussing tugs—cranes grabbing into barges—the pomp of Westminster. Somewhere in the soaring glitter of the building on the north bank was Rifkine's office. A thousand suburban backyards flashed by, exposing their tawdriness to indifferent travellers.

Inevitably his thoughts came back to Caroline. He fed the new feeling of antagonism as if it were necessary to him. Already he half-believed the fiction about her that he had created. What chance had he had with her anyway? It was easy enough to say to a man with a record—tell the truth about yourself to the people you meet and like. You did that and they dropped you as if you were leprous. And if you waited, finally it was too late. The fault was hers and not his. Her upbringing gave her a built-in sympathy with the law—not with those who broke it. Sure—she and her mother saw no harm in finagling their tax returns. It was a form of dishonesty they didn't recognise. Emptying Balaban's safe was different. Duplicity and expediency, that's what they meant by justice. Amateurs wrinkling their noses at the pros. The hell with her, anyway. She'd learn and if she didn't, she'd suffer. All that was left was to get rid of her so that she represented no threat. For the first time in many years, he had two things together. His liberty and fifteen thousand pounds. He meant to protect both.

The slowing train stopped with a telescoped clatter. The Land-Rover was parked outside in the station yard. He picked his way across frozen filth and opened the offside door. Not till his bags were in the car did he look at Scott's face. He knew at once.

" All right—what happened?"

Scott's voice was flat and hopeless. " You won't like this, Craig. She knows you pulled her into that trailer."

For an instant, the words produced nothing but stunned disbelief. He tightened his grip on the other's arm, forcing Scott's body round. His cousin moved his head up and down a couple of times. Usher relaxed his hold. His ears still retained the lingering shrillness of the train's parting whistle—the milling scramble of the cattle in the truck on the other side of the station concourse. The same porters were lounging just inside the entrance. Yet twenty seconds had made it another time and place. He brought his feet together, bending over them to ease the pain in his stomach.

" *How* does she know?"

Scott lifted both hands in a gesture of defeat. " Best I can make out, when we stopped to change the wheel. She re- cognised your voice. And if you think that's bad, the one o'clock news goes one better. They opened Balaban's safe this morning." He put the motor in gear, his rubber-shod foot slipping on the clutch pedal. The Land-Rover jerked **forward.**

Usher moved from a dream into reality. He found it difficult to concentrate on what Scott was saying. He had an uncanny sense of prediction. This was exactly what he'd told Balaban's widow. Suddenly nothing was sure any more. For all he knew, a cop had been at her elbow prompting her. His mind darted to the people in the train on the way down. Those business men with their crap about the Common Market—they could have been cops. When he left the coach at Andover, one of them had been missing. He twisted quickly in his seat, looking back at the empty dazzle of the road. His brain started to zigzag like a hare breaking cover.

"Did you see anyone near the house this morning—have there been any phone calls?"

Scott shook his head. "Your telegram—nothing else. No one's been near the place."

Usher relaxed. Jamie would know—the village was too small to hide signs of a raid. He replaced one source of apprehension with another.

"Can you remember what it was they said on the news—the exact words?"

Scott's answer was monotonous against the hiss of tyres on packed snow. "There was still no trace of the missing jeweller. Nothing about the girl. The guy said the safe was opened by the makers on police instructions. That's all. The word robbery wasn't mentioned."

Usher sat huddled. His clothes were a covering grown loose and chilly. He couldn't bring himself to use the girl's name. "They're stalling," he said loudly. "You're damned right they know what's missing. What about her —has she mentioned Balaban?"

"Once," said Scott curtly. "It's you that's on her mind. She's hostile. I've got a message for you." He repeated it.

Usher nursed the threat sombrely. It made him think of double gates in a twenty-foot wall. The long walk at night from Reception to the lighted cell-block. Three hundred cages—one of them empty and waiting for him. Time stretched out beyond with each day like the one before and that to come. At the end of it all, a fogged glimpse of himself, fifteen years from now. Hell—no—better take a rope. Either that or get rid of the only living witness. He saw her vividly in the fierce light of hate. He lifted his head from his hands, his face completely calm. It would need care to handle Jamie—to nurse him into acceptance of the inevitable.

"I suppose you've shown yourself?" He knew the answer instinctively.

Scott's hold on the steering wheel was tight. He defended himself doggedly. "You didn't expect me to go on pulling stockings over my head when she's recognised you. How long do you think it'll take the police to cable Ottawa —to find out we're cousins? When you go—I go with you."

The bitterness in Scott's voice gave Usher the clue he needed. Desperation to keep this house and land, the animals on it, had brought Jamie this far. If he could be convinced that he could still keep all this, he'd go the rest of the way. But it had to be done carefully. First he must think that he'd lost everything that mattered to him.

"I'm sorry," he said. "I know what this meant to you, Jamie. If it hadn't been for her . . . I'll call London— maybe the payment hasn't been made yet. If we're too late you'll have to clear your account in the morning." Not only hate itself but the need to hate was growing—as if his mind rejected an emotional vacuum. He prepared his ground with cunning. "All this belly-aching about me being a thief is just a cover—we'd better face that. If she could recognise my voice at twenty feet, through a trailer wall, she must have heard Balaban die."

The car went into a front wheel skid as Scott wrestled with the steering. His voice was shocked into sudden alarm.

"Jesus God! But she asked me what we'd done with him."

Usher's smile was thin. " She's playing it close to the chest. What did you expect her to say—' Assassin!' The fact remains—Balaban went out like a punctured pig," he lied. " If she heard one, she couldn't miss hearing the other."

The next seven miles were covered in silence. Scott came to life at the sight of the sawmill. He voiced his thought passionately. " I robbed the guy, Craig—but I had nothing to do with his death."

Already the whine of saw-torn wood split the air.

" Pull in here," said Usher. He waited till Scott manœuvred the Land-Rover on to the verge, then spoke with emphasis. " You better get this straight. If it ever comes to it, the law's not going to be interested in your good intentions, or mine either. Once she talks, they'll dig till they find a body. And when they've got that, there's a bunch of experts at the Public Prosecutor's Office to do the rest."

He didn't bother to judge the effect of his words but climbed back over the seat into the back. He crouched out of sight, hearing the motor slow in the village street. The car lurched up the lane, spinning in the drifts by the vicarage wall. The gate to the driveway was opened and shut. He stayed low till brushing straw told him they were under the barn. They carried the bags into the house. The hound rose from its bed, head towering above the kitchen table. Its tail lashed dangerously near the crockery there. Usher shed his coat and went into the sitting-room. He booted life into the fire, arching his ailing shoulder into the heat.

" Someone had better take a look at her," he suggested. As soon as Scott had gone, he retrieved the automatic from the drawer. He slid the clip out and in again, pumped a shell into the breech and set the safety-catch. The conversation upstairs was unintelligible but the girl's voice predominated. He heard the boxroom door close, his cousin coming down the stairs. Scott was moving his feet like a tired man.

Usher found the white streak in his hair with knowing fingers. "I just called London," he invented. "The money was paid into your account at eleven this morning. You'll have to do the best you can with your cheque-book. That means we go separately. I'm on an early flight."

Each phrase seemed to cost Scott an effort. "It looks as if you could be right. She's getting her kicks telling me how good her ears are. She's heard it all. The car, the horses, the church bells. Now she's guessing Sam's size by his bark. She says she wants to talk to you."

Usher held both hands to the flames, amazed at their steadiness. "She talks too much." The house stirred with its own sounds. Snow shifted on the roof, the clock was noisy in the hall. But the two men were quiet, sharing the thought of the woman upstairs—each mistrustful of the other's reaction.

Scott pulled a fresh bottle of Scotch from the drink cupboard. He frowned hard at the empty glass he was holding before quarter-filling it. The last half-hour had deepened the lines round his mouth. He spoke unhappily.

"She's your responsibility, not mine."

Usher watched the glass tipped and emptied. "Why don't we simply let her stay where she is. We could mail an anonymous letter to the cops from the airport."

Scott looked over the tilted bottle. He was treating the whisky like water.

"And have a reception committee, the moment we step off the plane! You're out of your mind. This crap about church bells is bluff. Right now she doesn't know where the hell she is. What do you want to do, tell her?"

Usher resurrected a spent match from the hearth. He started marking the brickwork of the chimney aimlessly.

"You don't want to go and you don't want to stay. What you really need is someone to hold your hand."

Scott's pupils were darker than usual—larger. He treated

the question solemnly. "And you never have, is that it? Neither the family—your friends—nor this woman. You'll get a good look at yourself one of these days, Craig. You know what you'll see—a middle-aged delinquent. And then it'll be too late."

Usher tossed the match on the logs. "I heard it all, twenty years ago. It didn't stop you coming to me when you were in trouble. It didn't stop me helping you. Now time's running out for both of us. Quit talking like your father. As for middle-aged delinquents, you joined them last Saturday."

Scott lifted his hands, his thin face resigned. "Just a couple of days—she'll be safe where she is if we're here—I can't pack a bag and walk out of here—there are animals."

Usher turned quickly, battering at the other's lack of logic. "That girl's going to put a rope round our necks, Jamie. I'm trying to save yours as well as mine but you won't let me. I'm going to be on that plane to-morrow morning."

A gate slammed in the stableyard. Scott drew the curtains an inch. "It's Parrish. I told him not to come to-night. I'd better go talk to him."

Usher came as far as the kitchen window. A light came on in the saddle room.

"Get rid of him," Usher ordered curtly. "Say what you like but get rid of him quickly." He waited behind the door, the safety-catch dropped on the automatic. The conversation across the yard was incomprehensible. Five minutes went by before Parrish trudged out towards the driveway. The lower half of his face was hidden by his upturned coat collar. His head was averted as he passed the house.

Usher reached the sitting-room in half a dozen strides. He poured himself a drink—a kingsize slub for Scott. He was back in his chair, his legs stretched out comfortably, when his cousin returned. Usher lifted his glass, looking through it at the colour of the flame in the fireplace.

"What's happened?" he asked quietly.

Scott's voice was slightly slurred. "He claims he didn't hear me tell him not to come—it's possible. I know what he thinks—that Lallie Mellor's here."

It was the moment for Usher to cast his line. He baited it with threat and promise, his voice insinuating.

"*Christ*, we're fools, Jamie. Think of it, she's the only witness against us. They couldn't get a conviction on your testimony—or mine. A confederate's word is no good without corroboration. We've buried Balaban. Put her out of the way and the penalty's no worse. But we go free. You could stay on here. Everything would be as it was a week ago—except you'd be fifteen thousand quid to the good."

Scott's arm hung suspended as if he'd forgotten it. His glass slopped as he put it on the tray. "Put her out of the way?" he repeated stupidly.

Usher's enlargement was inexorable. "Those paving stones will come up as easily as they did the first time. It'll be over in half an hour. You don't have to do a thing except give me a hand with a shovel. I'll take care of the rest."

He knew as he spoke that he was committed to a purpose he would fulfil.

Scott swallowed, his eyes uncertain. "That would be plain murder—you're not serious."

Usher's voice was soft. "Whatever you call it, there's no alternative, Jamie. I wouldn't put you wrong—there *is* no alternative."

Scott flushed under his tan. He steadied himself on the back of a chair and shoved the hair from his forehead.

"That means you'll need help. I've had too much Scotch," he added quickly.

Usher turned the watch on his wrist. "It's the shank of the day, Jamie—coming up six. Take a couple of hours' sleep. I'll brew some coffee and wake you."

He wrapped an arm round the other's shoulders and

helped him up the stairs. Scott stretched out in the darkened bedroom, eyes closed, his arms stiff by his sides. Usher threw a blanket over him and shut the door. He tiptoed across the landing. He heard the staccato of the girl's heels on bare boards. Her hands beat against the panelling.

" Open the door, Craig. I know you're there."

He took the key from the lock, turned abruptly and ran down the stairs. Back in the sitting-room, he wrenched the telephone wires from the wall. The hound jack-knifed from its place in front of the fire. It padded across the room to butt Usher's thigh gently. He looked at it uncertainly and then called the animal into the kitchen. The iron cauldron on top of the stove was full of rice and meat. He ladled a large ration into the dog's feed bowl. Then, pulling Scott's mac round his shoulders, he went out into the yard.

The trees bordering the driveway were wintry skeletons scarcely darker than the sky. The east wind had dropped, leaving the air pregnant with the promise of still more snow. He stared back at the house, intent on the boxroom skylight. Jamie's trip to the bottle had been providential. For a man who came of a line of whisky drinkers, he'd gone quickly. Nerves, judged Usher. He and Jamie had learned the use of Scotch along with salted porridge and, twelve times a year, the haggis. He could shut his eyes and feel the under-heated dining-room. The austere black furniture, sled-hauled four generations ago, when the Valley was a wilderness. He remembered the nightly terror of the ten unlighted steps from the main staircase to their bedroom. Their great-grandfather's portrait on the landing—bearded, fearsome and God. A trick of the artist had given the light-blue pupils the power to move as you crossed the landing. The house was a monument to the Scottish way of life. The blackened shield over the drawing-room fireplace set the tone for the occupants.

Nothing without Honour

He heard the words sing in his uncle's mouth—a chanted accompaniment to the downward swish of the ashplant.

He dismissed the memory and came back to his cousin. He'd wake Jamie with the thing done. There'd be no more than a sack to be lifted into the Land-Rover and buried. He considered his next move dispassionately. A shot fired through a silencer wouldn't be heard beyond the confines of the yard. He opened the main stable door and walked the dusty passage to the tool-room. Picks, shovels and crowbar were where Scott had laid them. Empty sacks hung over a beam in neat half-dozens. He chose those without stencilled markings, stuffed five into one. Water drained from the corners of the yard into a central grating. There'd be blood—no stains must be left. First, he'd go up and unlock her. Whatever she said, he'd accept like a shamed man ready for retribution. Her first thought would be to get out of the house. He'd offer to drive her wherever she wanted—to the cops if necessary. They'd come past Jamie sleeping and down the stairs, then out here. He'd be one pace behind her, the gun ready in his pocket. Then nothing. She'd never know what hit her.

He carried the tools over to the Land-Rover, came back and spread the sacks round the central grating. The initiative was still his. What the hell did the police have to go on? An empty safe and two missing persons. They wouldn't know who'd robbed whom. They couldn't be sure that the girl wasn't in the coup, or even Balaban himself. If they challenged him at the airport, they'd be bluffing. He'd carry nothing but a valid passport and a few pounds. He'd sink the gun, fifty miles away, twenty feet under water. There wasn't one single charge they could hold him on. The last details here were all-important. Every sign of her stay had to be destroyed. He'd go through that boxroom like a carpet-sweeper. Her brain was fast and clever. She was capable of stashing a handkerchief to be found later. He'd have to look for lipstick on the bathroom towels—the unwashed cups in the sink. Everything must be checked. And Jamie . . . Jamie'd be all right. It would be too late for him to do anything but go the limit.

He looked at his watch. Half an hour had passed since he left the house. By now, Jamie would be out like a light with that load of Scotch. It might as well be now as later. He stuffed the automatic in the right-hand pocket of the mac and walked over to the kitchen door.

: :                                        : :

Scott lay quite still in the darkness of his room, listening. The Scotch was a pool of warmth in his stomach. His pulse-beat was too rapid and his head rang. But the speed of his reflexes had lost nothing. He had heard Usher climb the stairs, the slither of his soles from one door on the landing to the other. For one moment, Scott thought his hand had been over-played down below. That Craig had noticed that last slopped drink—detected the fake signs of drunkenness.

He raised himself from the bed and padded out on socked feet. The light was on in the girl's room. He peered through the banisters into the hall. The lower half of the house was quiet. He soft-footed down the staircase, close to the wall to avoid creaking boards. The fire crackled on an empty sitting-room. The curtains were still drawn. His eyes traced the telephone wires wrenched from the wainscoting. He opened the table-drawer—the automatic was gone. He crept into the hall. Behind the closed kitchen door, the dog was noisy over a bone. Two pools of water on the parquet marked the place where his rubbers had been. His mac had vanished from its hook. He lifted the top of the deep chest, unearthing an old pair of flying boots and a flashlight. He carried them back upstairs and sat on his bed. The clothes he was wearing—these shoes—had to serve. There was no time to spend looking for something more suitable. He grabbed a heavy sweater. He was outside the boxroom before he noticed that the key was missing. His fingers brought hurried response.

" I'll have to find something to break the door down. Get your clothes on ready—leave nothing behind."

Downstairs in the sitting-room, he stood behind the curtains. Across the yard a light showed in the tool-room. He could only guess what Usher was doing there. He ran through to the kitchen and bolted the door on the inside. The hound, fed, warm and lulled by sight of the familiar— stirred comfortably. Scott took a meat-cleaver from the dresser. The oblong steel blade had the heft and weight of a machete. He stumbled up the stairs and attacked the box-room door. The noise of the blows reverberated, splintering the panels. The cleaver sank deep into the wood. Chips flew but the panelling held firmly along its joints. Chopping through half-inch timber would take forever. His head still buzzed but the warmth of the whisky seemed to have evaporated. He slugged hopelessly, the cleaver twisting in his sweating hands. Picking it up from the floor, he inserted the end like a wedge between door-jamb and wall. Plaster flaked off the faced stone. He abandoned all thought of caution. A third of the blade was sunk behind the metal box holding the tongue of the lock. The shadows of the girl's feet were spiderlike in the light under the door. He tried prising the jamb from the wall. It was no good. He needed more leverage. He ran into the bathroom searching for the metal bar he needed. There was nothing. A noise from outside took him to the window. Usher was crossing the yard with an armful—shovels, pick. He disappeared under the barn beside the Land-Rover. Scott was half-way to the boxroom when he remembered the cellar. He'd opened the last case of Scotch down there. He took the stairs down, four at a time.

He wrenched open the cellar door. The flight of stone steps were steep. A light would shine into the yard. He groped into dank cold air, bumping into the refuse of six years. Baled newspapers, bottles, broken furniture. In the far left hand corner he knelt down, moving his arms like a

161

swimmer using the breast stroke. Outstretched fingers touched the empty whisky crate, descended to the dirt-covered floor. He rummaged till he found the case-opener. He mounted the stairs, indifferent to the thud of his stock-inged feet. The four-foot jemmy sank into the niche he had made between jamb and wall. Leaning his weight on the implement, he wrenched with all his strength. Again and again till at last wood and iron cracked like a pistol-shot. The whole lefthand side of the door broke loose as the lock fell useless on the landing. He prised the jamb free and pulled the girl through the space. He pointed at the flying boots and sweater on the floor. Somewhere between his left eye and ear, a tiny hammer beat incessantly. He cleared his mouth of the taste of plaster.

" Get those things on—and make it fast."

She had tied her hair in a green scarf. She wore no make-up. Her face was pale, her eyes half their usual size. She dragged the sweater over her suède coat, put her shoes in her handbag and stepped into the boots he had given her. She looked at him, waiting for his next order. He gripped her wrist tightly and led her down the stairs. He cut the hall-light and dragged at the bolts of the unused front door. For a moment he stood, stock-still, interpreting the sounds outside. Then he opened the door cautiously. The spare crescent of lawn and neglected garden were trim under a white coverlet. The backs of the stables separated them from the yard. He whispered, trying to give his voice the authority it needed.

" We've got to cover a mile on foot. I can't drag you. Where I'm taking you, you'll be safe. Is that clear?"

Her eyes were level and searching. Her face cautious but unafraid. " What are you doing this for?"

He pulled the door quietly shut behind him. " Don't ask questions. All you have to know is that if Craig gets hold of you, you're finished."

On their left, snowflakes tumbled into the glow of the sitting-room curtains. Other than that, they were surrounded by an infinity of space where nothing moved. He had to get her as far as the Mellor house. Once there, he had to make sure he left her unable to put her threats into practice. What came next was anyone's guess. First he had to face Craig. He didn't even know what he'd say. That he'd put her on a car headed for London, maybe. With any luck, Craig would take the news as a signal to run; leaving him to work out his own salvation. And with it, her release.

There was a sudden battering at the locked kitchen door. He heard the hound's deep warning bark. Without speaking, the girl stretched out her hand. He took it and ran into the obscurity in front of them. They pounded across the lawn as far as the box-hedge surrounding the garden. He dragged her down in its shelter, looking back at the house. There was a crash of breaking glass—then one after another, the lights came on till the whole building was ablaze. The moment Craig discovered what had happened, his first thought must be to block the obvious escape route. He'd probably take the Land-Rover and try to reach the village before them. There was a mile of lane and driveway in which to do it.

Scott's eyes refocused, the shadow and whiteness around him gradually taking on meaning. He knew every hedge and wall on the property, each ditch now disguised as solid ground. They were facing north—in the opposite direction to the village. The Mellor house lay somewhere over his right shoulder. A broad sweep would take them to the sunken lane that led up to the gallop. Once this was crossed, only the river was between them and Mellor land. They stumbled on, stopping every fifty yards or so to free the clogged snow thickening their soles. He found the old badger break in the hedge unerringly, shouldered enough room free for her to pass. He dropped her down into the lane, to fall thigh-deep into the banked snow. They waded rather than walked to the other side. Taking her weight on his chest, he heaved her up on the bank. The slope descended sharply to where alder and willow drooped over the river. They slithered down the incline. He took a firm hold of a branch, testing the ice with a foot. It gave immediately, water running into his shoe. He jumped back, ducking as the released bough showered him with snow. He buttoned his coat high to the neck.

"We've got to get across this river. There's a bridge a quarter of a mile on. It's the only place. We'll be near the house."

Something broke cover on the far bank. She came close to him with an instinctive movement. He grabbed her arm as a dog-fox flashed left, brush held high.

"The house you just left," he explained. "I don't know where Craig is any more than you do."

The upper part of her body was shapeless under the baggy sweater. It was too dark for him to see her eyes but her voice was still controlled.

"Don't worry about me. I'll be all right."

Somehow the tone angered him. As if she had ranged herself on his side and wanted him to know it. The assumption was unwarranted. He pushed her in front of him, brusque with fresh mistrust. They followed the line of the willows along the bank. Across the narrow stretch of water, was the complete loneliness of the fir plantation. Three fields on, he picked out the glimmering shape of the bridge, fifty yards distant. If Craig's brain had worked fast enough, this could well be the ambush. He put his mouth to her ear.

"We cross there. There's a chance he's waiting for us. One wrong move and we've had it."

There was no catch in the throat—no drama—just the movement of her head in acquiescence. He crept forward, feet soundless on the snow. The white outline of the bridge arched into the shadowed trees. His eyes strained ahead. The hedge bounding the back paddock was a perfect hiding-place. His fingers found a couple of pebbles the size of golf-balls, worn smooth by the river. He straightened up and fired the stones, twenty yards apart. He dragged the girl down beside him. The missiles fell simultaneously. One smacked the stonework of the bridge—the other sank into the snow-girt hedge. They crouched, touching bodies motionless. The only sound was of water gurgling under the bridge where the river was not completely iced-over. He lifted his head towards Chestnut Gate. For a second he thought he was disorientated. Then he realised that every light in the house had been extinguished. Not even the silhouette of farm or stableyard showed on the hill-ridge. The place where they stood was part of the snowbound night. He put a hand in the small of her back, propelling her forward. They ran over the bridge, leaving the fastenings on the gate as they found them. Faced with the sombre avenue of trees, she found his hand again. He sensed the complete lack of coquetry in the gesture, the need of human contact.

" I'm frightened," she said very quietly. " I'm sorry. I'm suddenly frightened."

The tyre-tracks of the Land-Rover were obscured. His mind followed their route up to the deserted summer-house. His own fear made him irritable.

" Snap out of it. There's not much farther to go."

They broke into a jog-trot. He matched his stride to hers, husbanding his breath. The cold air had cleared his head. They climbed the long drag till at last the sweet lines of the Georgian house glimmered through the trees. He halted in the coachyard.

" I've got to break in here. It's empty but at least you'll be safe."

She ducked her head and was half-way across the yard before he caught up with her. His anger was mingled with a sense of injustice. She had no right to risk a life that he'd given her. He swung the flat of his hand hard across her cheek. Then he caught her by the elbows, half-carrying her to the wall. He pinned her there till he was able to control himself. He let her go suddenly, his voice hard with disgust.

" What's the use. I'm making a goddam fool of myself.

There's no point, going on like this. Go ahead and run if that's what you want."

She was holding her cheek, pressing herself against the wall. Her plea was barely audible.

" Please don't leave me here alone."

He looked down at the hand on his sleeve, finding it an affront. This woman could cling as readily as she could aim a knee at his groin. Everything was taken for granted—including one man's disloyalty to another.

" What am I supposed to do—walk you to the nearest police station?"

She edged a little closer. " I'll do whatever you say. But you can't leave me alone."

" Can't!" he exploded. " For Chrissakes what do you think this is—some kind of outdoor game?"

She took her hand from his sleeve, brushed it across her mouth.

" Not a game, no. I don't even know where I am. I'm afraid."

Again that word. He was spent with fatigue—haunted by the last ugliness of death in a pit he had helped dig.

" *You're* afraid," he said heavily. " Don't you ever think of anyone but yourself? Your troubles are over. You're alive, aren't you? A few hours and you'll be free. What about us—or doesn't your imagination carry you that far?"

The tenseness of her body was more explicit than any hysteria. " I know what you're thinking. But I swear I won't say a word to anyone. Not even to the police. If they ask me questions, I'll lie. But help me."

He gazed out at the dark huddled trees, uncertain whether he would have let her run.

" I've gone as far as I'm going for you," he said finally. " From here on you've got to help yourself."

" I'm not a fool," she answered steadily. " And I'm not ungrateful. Let me prove it."

The luminous hands of his watch gave him the hour.

Eight o'clock. "It's this or nothing. A locked room where you'll be out of harm's way. I'll stay for a bit. They'll come and get you when I've gone."

She put the question shakily. "Who will?"

He moved his shoulders. "The cops. Somebody, anyway. You've got my word for it."

She lifted her face. "It's a funny thing. You won't trust me yet I believe everything you say."

He smiled in the dusk, determined not to be hooked as easily as this. He shone the flash squarely on her. The chiffon scarf round her hair was a wet rag. The baggy sweater and flying-boots gave her the appearance of a small girl tricked out in her father's clothing. A small girl ashamed of her weeping. In spite of himself he was moved to sympathy. He voiced it roughly.

"Blow your nose. And your stockings are coming down."

She dragged the sleeve of the sweater across her eyes. "I never felt so miserable in all my life. Do you think I *care* how I look?"

He nodded. "Every woman does. All the time. Now stay in the doorway and don't move. I've got to find a way into this place."

She was almost humble. "Can't I come with you?"

He took her arm, pulling her into the shelter of the kitchen doorway.

"You said you were going to do as you were told. The neighbourhood hasn't had a haunting in a hundred years. If you see something rattling chains, give it the knee treatment."

He skirted the walls, looking for an unfastened window. They were all shut tight, secured on the inside by thumb-screws. He followed the length of a drain-pipe with his lamp. Three-quarters of its surface were enclosed in cement. The casing offered no hold to a would-be climber. He tried the cover of the coal-chute. Padlocked. He reconnoitred the broad front steps. The trees around him were hushed, smothered under a relentless weight of snow. The only gauge of distance was the occasional buzz of a car along the road to the village.

For a moment, she'd had him going. *I'm alone and afraid, sir. But I trust you.* Then the tears. She was a good performer. Anyone who could smile her way into a fortune had to be. He ran round the south wall to the greenhouses. He had to go in like the amateur he was. He had no time for refinements. The flashlight pierced cobwebbed panes, picked out the jungle of dead plants along the racks. The brick walk passed behind a rusted furnace and steam-coils. He raised the light. French windows gave entry into the house proper. He put an elbow through the nearest pane and undid the catch. The whole segment lifted up on a ratchet. He went back to the coachyard. She was huddled in the doorway where he had left her.

" Come on," he said. " We're in."

She stayed close to him. He helped her through the window and lowered it back in position. The air inside the greenhouse was sharp with the smell of rotting tubers. The disc of light passed over the floor. Rats had made confetti of yellowing newspaper. He felt her shiver. They followed the beam to the glass door. He shouldered her out of the way and used his elbow again. He pushed his arm through and turned the key. The breakfast-room was furnished after the manner of retired colonels, Indian Army. Uncomfortable, with tables and chairs of bamboo, cluttered with Benares brass. A Japanese screen swung in the sudden draught. He tried the door to the corridor. It was unlocked. The rooms beyond were alien and eerie under dustsheets. He backtracked to the servants' quarters, the girl by his side. A swinging baize partition gave access to a stone passage. Left and right were the sculleries and pantries. The kitchen outdid his own for size. Flagged, cheerless and vast, with stoutly-barred windows. It was as good a place to leave her as any. He flicked the light button on and off, tested the stove for current. A red eye glowed under the switch. Both power and light were still connected. He mounted a chair and removed the bulbs in the ceiling. There was no telling how long she would be here. There was water in the faucet. If she went hungry for a few hours, she wouldn't hurt. But without heat she'd freeze.

He explored the front of the house, collecting an armful of cushions from the drawing-room, a portable heater from the library. The flashlight flickered over stuffed bookcases, settled on the dark ugly desk. The upright telephone must be forty years old. He looked at it for a while, tempted. Then he lifted the ear-piece off the hook. His hand moved only inches. He remembered the wrenched wires in his sitting-room. A bell on the wall tinkled as he replaced the receiver. He was at the door when it sounded again, shrill and insistent. He hurried away. By the time he reached the kitchen, the last strident cry had ceased to echo through the house. She moved towards him with quick complicity, as though accepting the sound of the bell as a signal of common danger. He plugged in the fire, locked the passage door and pocketed the key. Then he looked at her sourly.

" Somebody pulled the wrong lever at the local exchange, that's all. Make yourself comfortable. This is home."

He opened the outer door, searching the coachyard. Already their footsteps were half-buried in fresh glistening whiteness. He closed the door and drew the flimsy curtains. She was sitting on the floor, struggling out of the sweater. She had left one cushion for him. Neither too near nor too far away. He squatted on it, watching the curve of her neck as she dragged off the flying-boots. She wrapped her legs in her skirt and held curled toes to the glowing bars.

In some strange way, both her silence and submissiveness offended him. In a little while, he had to face his cousin with an admission of disloyalty. He needed her voice even in attack. Anything so that he might answer and justify himself. She was hugging her knees, her eyes hidden by a swatch of candy-coloured hair. She turned suddenly as though sensing his state of mind.

" You're not going to care what I think. But I'll say it just the same. I'm sorry for you. Craig got you into this, didn't he?"

He held a cigarette to the red element. " I got myself into it. What about him—aren't you sorry for him, too?"

Her eyes were hidden again. " Craig's out of reach of anything I feel. That *anyone* feels. No. I'm not sorry for him."

He dealt sharply with the implicit sympathy. " Worry about yourself—we'll make out."

She buried her face in her hands, her voice muffled. " It's like a dream. A horrible dream and I don't understand it."

He joined battle gladly. " What *do* you understand? Hearts and roses—the good life in South Kensington. The groceries delivered every morning, for ever and ever, amen? What would you know about a guy like Craig?"

She pushed her fingers through her hair. " Nothing," she said with conviction. " Thank God, nothing."

He blew smoke at his feet. " Neither of you stood a chance together. Craig and I are the same flesh and blood. We grew up in the same house. I'll tell you about Craig. My father flogged him into an appreciation of something he never forgot. The shortest distance between two points is a straight line. That's the route he's taken ever since. Regardless. Count yourself lucky."

She moved deep into her own embrace, her tone bitter. " Regardless. Do you know what it's like to look at someone you've loved and feel nothing but hatred—you only stopped him killing part of me."

" You're ringing the wrong doorbell," he said. " I've got a limited knowledge of love."

She shifted on the cushions, looking up at him. " You must have. And women, too. It doesn't matter. Whatever you are, you know what pity is. But not Craig. You couldn't have done what he did. I'm certain of it."

" I'll tell you what you can be certain of," he answered.

"That I'm going to walk out of here, pretty sure I've done the right thing. But that's not saying I'm proud of it. In a straight choice—you or Craig—you'd be on the loser's end. I've lived too long surrounded by people like you to think they're worth a second thought."

She moved restlessly. "What do you mean by 'people like me'?"

He spared her nothing, remembering. "A smug bunch of hypocrites who'd tolerate Judas himself provided he was very O.K. Provided he didn't pick his nose and the neighbours didn't object. That's what I mean by people like you."

Her cheeks flamed redder than the heat of the fire warranted. "How can you say a thing like that? Is that why you hate yourself for saving my life? You don't really *want* gratitude, do you? That would prove you were wrong about me."

He ran a speculative hand across the stone floor. Age had polished the surface to smooth brilliance. He was suddenly tired of this aimless soul-searching. Reality was a dead man in a hole, a mile away.

"I'm going to give you a tip. You'll have a little time to think. Use it working up a good story for the cops. You're high on the list of suspects yourself."

She struggled to her knees. "That's not true. Mr. Balaban knows it isn't true."

Looking at her, he was certain that she was ignorant of the jeweller's death. Craig had to be wrong. He ground out his stub on the floor.

"Maybe. I'd have the story ready in any case."

Her eyes and mouth were grave. "The truth isn't hard to tell. Or don't you believe that either?"

It was time to lower the curtain on a lousy act. "And God's good as long as you pay your taxes. I'm off. You'll be out of here in a few hours. Do the best you can. So long." He climbed to his feet.

She watched him as far as the door, the hope patent that

even now he would change his mind and stay. Only when she was sure he was leaving did she speak. Her voice was very small but unafraid.

"Good-bye. Whatever you're looking for, I hope you'll find it."

He shrugged. It was an odd reward. "I'll try to remember. Meanwhile, I'll be putting as much distance between us as I can."

He walked out to the coachyard, locking the door behind him. He looked back through the chink in the curtain. She was hunched in front of the fire, her shadow spindly on the floor.

Along the carriageway and down into the trees would cut five hundred yards from the journey home. But the route passed close to the summerhouse. He trudged under the portico and forked left on the long beat back to Chestnut Gate. The avenue dropped through the firs. The darkness hung low above his head, encroaching on his footsteps. And always wet snow, sailing into his eyes and mouth. He crossed the bridge and ran clumsily up the slope of the back paddock. He unlatched the iron gate at the top. The lights were still out in the stables and kitchen. He crept under the barn, groping along the front of the Land-Rover. The radiator was cold. He trotted over to the back door. The curtain whipped in the broken window. He stepped inside quickly, taking the chill with him. He stood quite still for a moment. Then he heard Usher call. A slit of light showed across the hall. He turned the handle of the sitting-room.

His mind had always faced a man waiting in darkness—a hostile stranger with a gun in his hand. But Usher was sitting in a chair by the fire. The hound was at his feet. A tight strap round its nose prevented it from barking.

"Shut the door behind you." Usher's voice was expressionless.

Scott found his resolution shaken by the other man's composure. He walked over and unmuzzled the wolfhound.

172

It whined softly, foolish with pleasure. He chose the words with difficulty.

"I'm sorry, Craig. I had to do it."

Usher nodded. The bottoms of his trousers were steaming in the heat of the logs. He pushed a hand through his piebald thatch of hair. He watched Scott fondle the animal mechanically. Usher's mouth was derisive.

"You bloody fool. She always wanted a knight in shining armour. And see who gets tapped!"

The dog's coat was rough under Scott's fingers. He answered nervously.

"Why don't we skip the preamble? I couldn't hold still for another killing. That's all there is to it."

Usher's easy movement uncovered the gun concealed beneath his thigh.

"What the hell did you come back here for—to save the cops the trouble of looking for you?"

Scott's gesture was one of defeat. At the end of it all, you walked alone. He moistened his lips.

"You picked the wrong guy. I guess both of us knew it from the start. Maybe your way out was the right one. I just don't have the stomach for it."

Usher was sitting upright in his chair. "Do you know what I've been telling myself, sitting here. When he comes in that door, I'll empty this gun into his big stupid head."

Scott's eyes were level. "Why didn't you?"

Usher's face was suddenly old. "I've known you too long, Jamie. It's as simple as that. You're like all would-be heroes—when the chips are down you think with your feet. Now she's certain to talk. There'll be cops at her from the moment she's found. She's *got* to talk to save herself. And you have to leave her a mile away from your own house."

Scott's hand stopped half-way to his pocket. He completed the gesture automatically, shucking a cigarette from the battered pack. Trust Craig to call every shot. A would-

173

be hero posturing in a useless sally. He kept his eyes on the
spent match, unwilling to raise them.

"I might have known."

Usher came to his feet, pacing with a cat's delicate
menace. He neither gloated nor condemned.

"Twenty yards behind you from the bridge to the house.
But don't feel bad about it. I've been at this caper a long,
long time. I could have dropped either of you fifty times."

The thought ran like a train of gunpowder. Scott raised
his head.

"Why didn't you? It would have solved a lot of problems for you."

Usher came to a halt, his pale-blue eyes hooded. "Why?
I'll be asking myself that question for the next ten years—if
I last that long. Do you realise what's going to happen
when the law finds her? They'll move into this neighbourhood with dogs and bulldozers, looking for Balaban. They'll
upend the whole village till they find where he's buried."

Scott carried the reminder to the fireplace. However they
would frame the indictment, this wasn't robbery any more
but murder. The word that brought every stranger out in
pursuit till the last hiding place was sealed off.

He answered painfully. "She's got no idea that Balaban's dead. I'd stake my life on it."

"You already have." Usher's pupils focused as if Scott's
face were long to be remembered. "I don't know if you'll
understand this, Jamie. The other night I said as a kid you
were nine feet tall for me. Now suddenly it's the other way
round. It's a funny thing—all that time I've been nursing
the idea that there was one guy I'd never lied to. Somehow
it mattered. This last couple of days I've fallen off the
wagon twenty times. I'm glad you came back. I hoped you
would."

Scott searched the other's face for a solution. "It's a
matter of time before they get us—isn't that it?"

Usher's expression was sardonic. "You're just a snotty-
nose in knee-breeches. I'm going to tell you what it'll be

like on the run. You'll die every time you go through a
frontier. You'll have no friends—only question-marks in
your head. After a while you'll get careless. A hot sun—a
drink. You'll be ten thousand miles away. People forget,
you'll think. But not this, Jamie. This they won't forget.
There'll be a warrant out for you as long as you breathe.
That's what you're going into."

A log collapsed in the grate. The dog's head lifted.
Scott moved from a scorching blaze. At least he was no
longer alone.

"And what are *you* going to do?"

Usher smiled. He looked almost happy. "I'm going to
run till I drop. I've got fifteen thousand quid in a Swiss
bank and two legs."

Firelight softened the shabbiness of the room. The dog
laid its head between its paws. Scott took last stock of it
all. From a prison cell, none of it would mean anything.

"I'm running too," he said simply.

It was a while before Usher replied. "Get a bag and
your passport. Rifkine can handle your dough. We'll take
the Land-Rover and cut across country to Reading. We
ought to make London Airport before midnight. I know
a place you can cash a cheque. We'll get the first plane out
—anywhere. Paris, Rome, Berlin. All we need is a head
start—we'll run them into the ground."

The automatic was still on the chair, the silencer glinting
in the light. Scott picked it up. It chinked against
the heavy key in his pocket. He spoke very seriously as if
this were the heart of the matter.

"I'm dumping this, Craig. The first running water we
see."

Usher was already lacing his shoes. He looked over his
shoulder. "Deep, Jamie. Deep. The spirit's willing but
the flesh is weak."

# CAROLINE WOODALL

She lowered the window. The snow was deep on the sill outside. Iron bars were sunk in the masonry, spaced deceptively. Head and shoulders seemed to pass then were firmly trapped. In the middle of her first attempt to go through she had heard the telephone ring. She struggled free, ran to the door and pounded on it with both hands. The bell stopped suddenly—as if the caller had grown tired of waiting. She lay shaking on the cushions, biting her fingers against the clamour in her head.

No picture came singly—only a confused impression of faces and voices. She fought her way out of the jolting darkness inside the horsebox and concentrated on the thought of escape. Again and again she returned to the window, extricating herself from the grip of the bars at the last moment. The woodwork round the lock was gashed where she had worked ineptly with a kitchen knife. Now the blade bent and snapped as she dug at the rusted screws.

She whirled at the sound of a car's motor, retreating to the farthest corner. She flattened herself against the whitewashed wall, trying to make herself small. A door opened at the front of the house. She heard men's voices. Taking hope in both hands, she ran towards the sound, shouting. Footsteps were hollow along the corridor—then silence. Her fists beat on the panels. A man cleared his throat importantly.

" Better let me do this, Major. Open the door !"

She leaned against the stonework, exhausted. " I can't. It's locked."

The second voice was cultured, the sibilants a little slurred.

176

"There's a spare set of keys in the scullery. I'll get them."

She stood in the open doorway, dazzled by the brightness of the naked bulb overhead. The oval blur grew features— a heavy jaw, soft colourless hair, pink eyes that showed hostility. The man's shoulders were bulky in cheviot tweed. He was tapping his crowded teeth with a signet ring. She looked at the uniformed policeman with relief. Conscious of her stockinged feet, she found her handbag and her own shoes. She propped herself against the wall and slipped them on.

Mellor's stride sandwiched her between himself and the constable. He donned a pair of spectacles, pivoting as he surveyed the kitchen, the cushions on the ground. He came close enough to her for his gin-loaded breath to register.

"What are you doing here?"

She sensed the animal threat by instinct and moved away. She tied the belt on her suède coat, hurrying her plea to the constable.

"I've got to see someone in charge—quickly."

Mellor picked up one of the flying-boots. He draped the sweater over an arm like a salesman, displaying it thoughtfully.

"What do you make of it, Allen?"

The constable tried the locked door to the coachyard. He pushed back his cap, his expression baffled.

"There's windows broken, miss. An entry's been effected. Are them boots yours?"

Mellor spoke contemptuously. "Of course they're not hers, Allen. Use your head, man. Where *is* your boyfriend—or are there several?" His smile was unpleasant.

She took the three steps to Allen's side, her voice ragged. "Why are we wasting time—*please* take me to the police station."

The words whipped into the constable's thinking like a command. He raised himself ponderously on his toes.

" I shall have to get other instructions about this, Major. You stay where you are, miss."

She ran a few yards along the corridor after him, fighting off Mellor's grasp. His fingers locked round her wrist. His mouth came near her ear.

" Don't worry about him. You and I can arrange this if you're sensible."

She moved quickly, wrenching off her right shoe. She held it by the toe and brought the spiked heel hard down on Mellor's hand. He dropped her wrist, his face ugly. She ran blindly towards the front of the house, flinging the baize door at the noise of pursuit. She waited in the shadow, listening to the constable's slow voice on the telephone. She stayed near Allen all the way back to the kitchen. He was obviously content with his news.

" I've got to take her into Central—that's the superintendent's orders."

Mellor's lips were as white as the surrounding skin. He was kneading the sinews on the back of his right hand.

" I'll drive you. I want this woman charged."

He was last out of the house, shutting off lights and fastening the door with a parade of ownership.

She settled herself in the back of the Bentley. She felt Allen's prim withdrawal as her knee touched his. Mellor handled the heavy limousine like a weapon, hurling it through the gates, dangerously near the stone pillars. He flicked on the radio, drumming out the beat on the steering-wheel. The shape of his neck—the slightly pointed ears —both fascinated and repelled her. She tried to think what she must do, remembering the collapsing door of the box-room—the thin lined face of the man who had rescued her. His bitterness had come close to the truth. Her mother's reactions were sure in face of potential scandal. Tight-closed ranks but behind them a constant needling—a reminder of disgrace dragged into the quiet Kentish country-side. Of motherhood martyred by a daughter's thought-lessness.

She stared out at the white rush of landscape, seeing nothing. They'd say she was young and Craig worthless anyway. They had a formula that took care of everything but the dull pitiless ache deep in her memory. She knew nothing of their justice—this was something more personal and primitive. The need to punish deliberate cruelty. Craig must suffer for what he'd done to her.

Sight of the town's first lights straightened the constable's spine. He stubbed his cigarette carefully into the ash-tray. Both hands were on his knees as the Bentley stopped for traffic signals. His pose was unbending for the curious eyes on the sidewalk.

The police station lay behind the Town Hall, a modest brick building with a hanging blue lantern. A notice board outside displayed Foot and Mouth warnings. Mellor parked squarely in front of the entrance. He swivelled round to give the girl the full value of his facetiousness.

"You recognise the architectural scheme, no doubt."

The constable's hold on her sleeve was loose but cautious. "Up the steps, miss. First door on your left."

She had an impression of firelight on brightly polished linoleum—an institutional clock on a drab wall. Behind a tall desk was a youngish sergeant, hatless and smelling of peppermint. He slammed the cover on his day-book and retrieved his tongue. Allen's salute was perfunctory.

"The Super, Sarge. We're expected."

The sergeant rapped on a door. C.I.D. was painted in black. He turned the handle gingerly then motioned them inside. She walked by his frank stare with dignity. The door closed behind them. The only concession to comfort was a bucket-shaped chair with worn horsehair stuffing. A shaded lamp had been dragged low above the untidy deal table. The man behind it was buttressed on thick splayed legs. The two bottom buttons of his waistcoat were undone, releasing the beginning of a sizeable belly. The planes of his head were sharp. Heavy eyebrows met over a shrewd appraisal.

179

Allen pulled himself to approximate attention. "This gentleman's Major Mellor, sir. Lily—that's Miss Hawthorne at the Exchange—got a signal from his house about an hour ago. She rang back but nobody answered. Then she telephoned the major. She knew the house was supposed to be unoccupied. I come over there with him. We found this young lady locked in the kitchen. Entry'd been effected through a window in the greenhouse, sir."

Mellor perched on a corner of the table. His tone was easy and confidential.

"It's simple enough, Superintendent. There are valuables in the house though we don't live in it for the moment. We arrived before they had time to ransack the place. The man with her must have heard us coming and cleared off. She's got some cock-and-bull yarn about having been taken there by force."

She swayed, feeling the sticky heat rise to her neck. She knew that if she could get through the next few seconds, she wouldn't faint. The superintendent whipped a chair under her and unfastened the top of her coat. She leaned back with closed eyes. She heard him call to the sergeant outside.

"A cup of tea from the canteen, Steve. Hot, strong and quick."

She shook her head at his inquiry. The crisis was past. Taking out her mirror with trembling fingers, she traced the outline of her mouth with lipstick. *Every woman cares how she looks.* The words seemed to mock her.

The superintendent's question was pointed. "Well, miss?"

She answered steadily. "My name is Caroline Woodall. I work for Mr. Balaban, a London jeweller. We were kidnapped two days ago—on the racecourse at Epsom."

Mellor offered his gold cigarette-case without success. He laughed outright. Somebody knocked on the door. The Superintendent balanced the saucer on the cup and put the tea by the girl's side.

"If that's your car outside, Major, you'll have to shift it. You're blocking the entrance."

"I think that can wait," Mellor said casually. "I'm preferring a charge of breaking-and-entering against this woman. You've your own man as witness."

The superintendent walked round the table. There was an edge to his politeness.

"I give the orders in here, Major. There's no need to detain you any longer. I'll send Allen home in one of our cars."

Mellor frowned. "I've an idea you're biting off more than you can chew. The chief constable's a personal friend of mine."

"He's also a policeman. We'll be in touch with you if it's necessary, sir. Good night." The superintendent shepherded Mellor to the door. She heard his hurried instruction to the sergeant. "Get me the Yard, Steve. I'll take it out there."

She gripped the cup tightly, transferring its warmth to chilled fingers. Allen was still at attention, his face blank. She looked beyond him to the hanging raincoat, the shapeless trilby on the hook above it. A clipped sheaf of WANTED notices was suspended next to a seedman's catalogue. On the edge of the table was a snapshot of two overweight children. The door opened. The superintendent jerked his head at Allen. Once they were alone, he sat down facing her. He was pushing a pencil from one hand to the other.

"Some officers are coming down from London. With this weather I can't say how long they'll be. You understand that you'll have to stay here till they arrive?"

She moved her head. "All right. *You* don't believe I've done anything wrong, do you?"

His eyes were kind. "Don't worry about anything. You don't have to make a statement but it'll help us and save time. Then we'll get a message to your family—let them know you're safe."

181

She heard the tick of the clock on the wall outside, the lowered voices of the men in the next room. She clutched the superintendent's wrist firmly.

" Have you found Mr. Balaban?"

He let her hand stay where it was. " Not yet—but we will. These men that abducted you—how many of them did you see?"

She felt the tears scald then roll. " Two."

His voice was soothing, almost hypnotic. His free hand moved towards the phone on the table.

"You just take it easy. Try to remember all you can about them."

She answered haltingly. " One's called Craig Usher. The other one I don't know. But they're leaving the country."

He was already spinning the dial. " Keep talking, miss. Anything at all you can think of might help. Their clothes —the way they talk—anything at all." He relayed her answers into the open line, his own voice urgent. Then he replaced the receiver.

She held the cigarette to the match he offered her. " Shouldn't I tell you from the beginning?"

He smiled. " If it'll help. Don't hurry yourself and don't be afraid."

She sat for a while, remembering. She started in a hard brittle voice that didn't belong to her.

" I suppose it must be nine months ago—some people asked me in for drinks . . ."

She stopped suddenly. Laying her head on the table, she covered her ears with her fingers and said no more.

# JAMES SCOTT

A hundred speakers reproduced the prim voice in bars, restaurants and lavatories.

"British European Airways announce the departure of Flight 165 for Paris. Will all passengers holding green boarding cards please go immediately to Channel 5 for customs and immigration formalities." The woman repeated herself in French.

23 : 35. Scott slid from the stool. In spite of the hour, the great hall was still busy. People dozed on the benches in front of the closed banks. A man cradled a querulous child, stilling its cries with awkward fondling. He held it up, displaying the chains of coloured paper, the plastic cherubs, a giant star in aluminium foil. The summons had assembled the usual complement of voyagers. Americans with young-old faces, the men lopsided under gadgets slung on shoulder straps—the women demonstrating good legs and close-fitting hats set on blue hair. The Englishmen wore suède shoes and their wives' expressions were distant. The Continentals, shorter in stature, burrowed their way to the head of the queue, impervious to unspoken criticism. The inevitable mystery-symbol wore mink and dark glasses. She moved with elegant restraint, a Hermes travelling case under her arm.

Scott took his place behind her. Usher's brindled head was half-way along the queue. They had bought separate tickets on the under-booked night-flight. From the moment they had reached the airport, neither had spoken or shown sign of recognition.

The tall hostess dammed the line at the doorway. She checked boarding-cards. The holders went right or left to where men sat at desks in the deserted Customs Hall. The file moved ahead rapidly. A man near Scott with the strained features of an insomniac was complaining loudly about plumbing. He seemed to hold his wife personally responsible for household inadequacies. The Canadian edged after the mink coat, the woman's scent sharp in his nostrils. He counted those left in the bay. A man in a grey Homburg, two youngsters in ski-clothes, his neighbour and Usher.

The hostess was saying the same thing over with tired courtesy. " British and Commonwealth passports to the right—others to the left, please."

Scott thumbed the cover on his own identification. The picture was five years old, taken that first year at Chestnut Gate.

James Scott. Born, 11 August 1918, York Mills, Ontario.

He looked up into the unfathomable eyes of the woman in the mink coat and closed the booklet hurriedly. The boy and girl forked left, their legs trim in elasticised ski-pants. Scott watched Usher lope across the hall to the desk. He saw the hand outstretched, the brief inspection and nod. It was all over in twenty seconds. Usher disappeared into the Transit Lounge. The hostess's smile revealed a smear of lipstick on her right canine.

"That's your ticket, Mr. Scott. I need the boarding-card."

He walked the thousand miles to the small desk. The man's face behind was out of the shaft of green-shaded light. The hand that took his passport wore a buffed signet-ring on the wrong finger. The official made a pencil mark against the passenger list. His voice was indifferent.

" Thank you, Mr. Scott."

His passage to the Transit Lounge was deliberate, anticipating a belated challenge that never came. Usher was deep in an arm-chair, legs crossed, his eyes half-closed. He cocked one thumb in sign of victory.

Scott mounted a bar-stool. Seasonal-wrapped whisky was offered at duty-free prices. Tiny figures with cotton whiskers sledded the length of the Gift Shop counter. 23.45. Another twenty minutes before take-off. He ordered a large Scotch, barely weakening the mixture with water. Beyond the plate-glass windows, a covered ramp led down to the tarmac. The runways were dotted with coloured lights. Mounds of plough-shifted snow glittered under the arcs. A ground-crew in wet slickers groomed and replenished the waiting Comet.

Scott lifted his glass, his gesture meaningful. He saw Usher's answering grin in the mirror. The clock hand jerked in pursuit of the seconds. 24:05 24:07 24:09. Then the quarter-hour. Flight departure was already ten minutes overdue. Suddenly the telephone rang by the exit to the ramp. The hostess transmitted the call over the p.a. system.

" British European Airways regret to announce a delay in the departure of Flight 165 to Paris, due to technical reasons. A further announcement will be made in half an hour's time. Light refreshments will be served to passengers on presentation of their boarding cards."

Scott was already on his feet. He looked round cautiously. Usher's raised shoulder signified indifference. The insomniac was first to reach the hostess. Scott heard the apologetic reply.

" I'm sorry, sir. That's the only information I have."

The man's tone hardened. " It never fails, does it? You get us out here three-quarters of an hour before it's necessary. Then we're told there's a delay. Technical reasons be damned. B.E.A. aren't down to one plane, surely. It's the middle of the night and I'm under doctor's orders. Not only that—people are meeting me in Paris."

The Continentals moved nearer, caught by the promise of drama. An American said something about manners. The woman in mink was still inscrutable behind tinted lenses. Usher's expression was bored.

The hostess smiled painfully. "We'll do whatever we can, sir. We can get a message by phone to your friends if you like."

The banality of the scene reassured Scott. He followed Usher into the lavatory. His cousin was bending over the hand-basin, drinking from the faucet. He straightened up, peering into the mirror. He brushed the piebald hair carefully with his hands.

"For God's sake, relax. You're home and dried. This sort of thing happens all the time. She can't move a yard till the law gets that letter."

Scott had addressed the cheap envelope to Scotland Yard on the train up from Reading. He made no attempt to disguise his handwriting. Since then his mind had emptied his inside pocket on the Immigration Officer's desk, a dozen times. He'd watched quick hands tear open the envelope— hard pebbly eyes scan the contents.

Usher turned round. "Mail it, Jamie. It'll make you human. There's a box outside. And keep away from me till we're through French customs."

Scott dropped the letter in the mail chute with a sense of finality. It would reach the Yard by second delivery. Noon and she'd be out of the house. The insomniac had cornered the hostess over by the bar. Their discussion continued. 24:30. Scott walked over to the door to the ramp. The Comet was illuminated—the ground crew busy with the baggage hatches. He turned as a new voice came over the p.a. system. A youngish man was in front of the mike. He wore a B.E.A. brassard on the left sleeve of his sports jacket.

"Will all passengers on Flight 165 go through to the Customs Hall, please."

The announcement pulled like a magnet, emptying the lounge. Scott found himself in the middle of the rush for the passage, impelled by those behind. Sixty-two men and women surged into the great hall. The exits were closed— every light in the place blazed. Half a dozen men in dark suits were grouped in the centre. One joined the airline official to block retreat to the passage. The others positioned themselves strategically. A short man called for silence. He had grey hair and an authoritative manner.

" I want you to listen to me carefully. I am a police officer attached to New Scotland Yard. You won't be detained long but I'd like your co-operation. As I call your names from this list I want the men to line up in front of me—the ladies stay where they are. Mr. and Mrs. O'Donnell. Mr. and Mrs. Starret. Mr. Duhameau . . ." He waited patiently while somebody translated. The Frenchman shrugged philosophically and took his place.

Usher was only feet away. The skin was stretched tight over his jaw-muscles. He seemed to hang from an invisible hook. Arms loose, the upper part of his body slightly out of perpendicular. He joined the line, stepping like a cat through water.

Scott shifted his weight, wiping his palms surreptitiously as his name was called. The inspector stuffed the passenger list in a pocket and snapped thumb and finger. A door opened. Caroline Woodall came out, moving with the blank stare of a sleepwalker. The inspector touched her arm.

" Go down the line, miss. If you see anyone you recognise, just tap him on the shoulder. No need to speak—just a tap on the shoulder." He stayed close to her as she started her long walk.

Scott was standing quite still. She had to reach him before she came to Usher. He hadn't known it would be like this. There was no more fear, even a sort of relief. He looked down at his feet, hearing the asthmatic breathing of the man beside him—the slow click of the girl's heels as she came nearer. His heart beat in his head as he raised it. She seemed smaller than he remembered, the thin fine lines tight about her mouth. The green suède coat was still stained with mud and whitewash. She hesitated no more than a fraction of a second. Then looking him full in the

187

face, she passed on. As she came to Usher, she stretched out her hand. He danced away from her like a quarterback, sidestepping past the men guarding the passage. The Customs Hall erupted into shouted confusion. Police whistles shrilled in the distance.

Scott's stumbling run took him with the others to the Transit Lounge. He forced his way through the crowd at the window. A plane was taxi-ing over the tarmac outside, its fuselage insignia vivid in the brilliance of the arcs. Suddenly Usher appeared, running with rolling head and flagging legs. More police whistles sounded off to his left. Rising on his toes like a man preparing to dive, he dashed headlong into the port engine of the moving airplane.

Even through half-inch plate glass, noise of the impact was stark. It froze the onlookers to complete immobility. For a moment there was no sound. A woman's shriek was the solvent. People milled like ants whose nest is disturbed, their faces shocked and disbelieving.

Only Scott was left at the window. He watched as an ambulance screamed across the tarmac. Already men were shovelling sand on the bloodstained snow. White-coated attendants loaded blanketed bundles into the back of the ambulance. He turned away, fighting the nausea in his stomach. Uniformed police were moving through the crowd, stolid and reassuring. His neck covered with sweat, the inspector was talking urgently to the hostess. She picked up the mike, nodding. Her voice was tremulous.

"B.E.A. announce the departure of Flight 165 for Paris. Will all passengers please proceed to Gate 5 for immediate embarkation."

Scott's slow walk took him past the place where Caroline Woodall stood surrounded by plain-clothes men. She lowered her eyes as he passed but not before he read the desolation in them. Then the cold wind of freedom was on his face.

⟩⟩⟩ If you've enjoyed this book and would like to discover more  great vintage crime and thriller titles, as well as the most exciting crime and thriller authors writing today, visit: ⟩⟩⟩

# The Murder Room
## Where Criminal Minds Meet

**themurderroom.com**

www.ingramcontent.com/pod-product-compliance
Ingram Content Group UK Ltd.
Pitfield, Milton Keynes, MK11 3LW, UK
UKHW040435280225
455666UK00003B/90